All that Glitters
JANE BRADFIELD

Mary, You know who you are!

Jane Bradfield

Copyright © 2010 Jane Bradfield
jb3cmr@gvec.net
All rights reserved.

ISBN: 1453733825
ISBN-13: 9781453733820

All that Glitters

All that glitters is not gold, –

Often have you heard that told.

Shakespeare: Merchant of Venice

For those I love
You know who you are

Chapter 1
1783

I dug my parents' grave by myself, the hard land resisting every stroke of the shovel. After they died of the pox within minutes of each other, I gently closed their eyelids.

They could never bear to be apart, so I lay them together as though asleep in each other's arms. Then I covered their beloved faces with a cloth and filled the grave with clods of earth. I slept all night atop their grave, my tears soaking the rough ground.

I left at dawn.

Only one relative, Cousin Emilie, cared about me. I had to find her. It would be at least a three-day walk to Versailles, but I couldn't think of anything else to do. I wasn't yet strong enough to make it to Paris. Maybe

I could have bribed a coachman, but I had nothing to bribe anyone with. I had my father's gold ring with the family crest upon it, but I would never part with that. I wore it tied around my neck in a velvet sack well hidden beneath my coarse shirt.

It was a hard journey, days on the rutted roads; nights huddled in musty fields under whatever cover I could find. Surrounded by field grass that made me sneeze, I hoped sniffling wouldn't reveal my hiding place.

At last, I approached Versailles. A great coach rumbled past me. I stepped aside to keep from being run over. A guardsman opened magnificent black iron gates decorated with gold. I followed in the coach's wake. Beyond was the château of Versailles, the heart of the kingdom. It took my breath away. The cobbled vista seemed to go on forever. Vast long wings, open spaces, acres of pale stone buildings...

Emilie was one of the salad makers of the King. Which of the vast wings of Versailles held the kitchens? I had almost given up searching when I heard banging and clanging and felt a rush of heat as a door was thrown open.

Great haunches of meat turned on spits over smoldering fires. The scent of pork, beef, and lamb was overpowering. I had never seen so many people. Hundreds. How could I spot Emilie in such a crowd of busy workers?

I wandered around for a long time and was about to give up when I heard, "Whatever are you doing here, Jacques?" I whirled around. Emilie wiped sweat from her brow with the back of her hand.

"Maman and Papa..." I swallowed. "...dead of the pox."

Emilie grabbed my shoulders and pushed me toward a window. She stared at me. "You had it, too, though your face is not badly pitted. You're still a handsome lad."

I held back tears. No one had spoken to me for a week, not even as I walked the muddy roads. I had begged bread from an old woman, but she said nothing. She had torn off a small chunk from her dark loaf, handed it to me with her gnarled fingers, and waved me off. I had drunk all the water I had brought with me and might have died of thirst had I not come across a small stream.

Eying a nearby cauldron, I asked Emilie, "Would you...could you...?"

"Bless me, of course. It's just some clear broth. Is that all right?"

Is that all right? As if I'd spent years being a picky eater. I'd even subsisted on chestnut gruel, for goodness sake.

When she brought me the broth, I saw Emilie had some flour in her curly hair. She must have passed too close to a pastry chef. If one of the starving peasants had seen it, he'd have licked it right off her head.

When I finished, Emilie offered another serving, but I declined. Food after days with little to eat can make one's stomach bounce.

Emilie took a corner of her apron and blotted a drop of broth from my chin. "What are your plans?"

"To find work. Hopefully, here."

She walked to a sink, took out great handfuls of lettuce and laid them to drain on some linen. Then she dried her hands on her apron and returned to me.

"I don't think you'll have to muck out the stables. You're smarter than that. I have an idea...." Emilie grabbed some kitchen shears and led me to a storage room overflowing with sacks of onions and grain.

"Sit down."

"Where?" There was scarcely room to stand.

"On that onion sack," Emilie said as she went to a corner and rummaged through a bag.

"I've been saving these cast offs to make a dress out of, but I can spare some. Here, put these on." She handed me a waistcoat, a frockcoat, knee breeches, and stockings, then turned her back. I struggled with the white stockings I'd seen footmen wearing. I thought the knee breeches ridiculous, but I supposed if you were going to work in a grand château... "All right, you can look."

She squinted in my direction. "You'll do. Take them off."

"I just put them on."

She rummaged in another corner and handed me a bar of soap. "Find some water and wash up. Don't forget your hair." She reached out to touch my matted brown hair, but drew back as though nits might jump onto her hand.

"When you're clean, put on only the stockings and knee breeches. Then come back to me."

Emilie left to pat the greens with the linen towel. I did as I was told, hiding the velvet pouch with my father's ring in the folds of the frockcoat.

"Ow!" I said when Emilie had me in her clutches.

"Sorry," Emilie said as she cut my hair with the shears. She held my chin, turned it to face her and clipped the hair hanging in my eyes into bangs. Emilie tousled my hair and stood back to admire her work. She took a discarded garment from her sack and brushed the clippings from my shoulders. "Finish dressing. I have to get back to work."

When I walked out of the storeroom, she was dunking another load of lettuce into the sink.

She sensed me behind her and turned. There were tears in her blue eyes. Emilie tried to wipe them away. She was mourning my parents, but she didn't want me to know. People died all the time. Medicine was blind man's bluff. You almost always died if you got the pox. Only a few survived it—marked by the scars the pustules left.

Emilie took her apron and blotted the tears from her cheeks. She looked me over. "Quite grand you are.…"

My stockings were a trifle long, so I hitched them higher. That didn't seem to bother her, but something else did. "Shoes…I'll have to work that out."

The day I set out for Versailles, I had worn my father's shoes. My feet grew too fast to buy a pair with the meager income we lived on from our share of the crops. My father's shoes, by the time I made it to Versailles, looked as if I had shredded them with a fork.

"Go now into the great halls and do anything anyone asks of you," Emilie said. "I haven't the authority to hire anyone, but I can give you food. If someone notices you have no shoes, say they were muddy and you'll get them as soon as they dry."

I began my first day of work in my stocking feet.

Than night, I slept on onion sacks in the storeroom. "I'll bring you a blanket tomorrow," Emilie said.

I had tried to sleep on the grain sacks, but they made me sneeze.

෴

Chapter 2

I was the son of a minor nobleman who had done the unforgivable. He fell in love with my mother. She was the daughter of the peasants who worked the land for my father's family.

She was beautiful, of course. But I don't think that was the reason my father fell in love with her. I think he loved her because she listened to him. She had a wonderful stillness about her. Both my father and I would stop being jittery the moment we looked into her honey colored eyes.

My grandparents were so enraged that my father fell in love with a peasant that they refused to acknowledge my existence. Not just my birth, mind you. My existence.

When my parents died, I knew better than to go to them. After my father was thrown out of the manor house, he and my mother were allowed to live on the property in a peasant cottage with a thatched roof. Hoping that I had the strength to make it to Emilie after their death, I closed the creaking door of the only home I had ever known.

Emilie was the daughter of my mother's sister, who had died having Emilie. Emilie wasn't calm like my mother, but that was fine with me. We used to race through the fields, startling our lone milk cow. I always won. Her legs were longer than mine because she was a few years older, but I was faster.

∽

Chapter 3

Sometimes the yapping little dogs of the King's old aunts would break free of their quarters and chase the capuchin monkey around the *Galarie de Glaces*. Pretending to round up the spaniels, I chased them, the candle stubs in my sack bumping against my legs. I was really zigging and zagging for the fun of it. The fun never lasted long, of course. A grown-up wearing a long face would stop it. Then I had to round up the dogs and carry them to the old aunts' quarters. I held a dog beneath each arm, and the monkey bounced on my shoulder as I held his broken chain. If the spaniels had weighed one more ounce, I couldn't have managed.

If you've spent most of your life being hungry, prying candle stubs from the King's candelabra was a small price to pay for a bowl of stew.

I wasn't a ceremonial candlesnuffer. That was too grand a job for the likes of me. I didn't mind that someone else got the duty of seating new candles every day. The King had hundreds of candelabra! Every night, I turned the candle stubs over to another servant. I suspected he sold them to peasants to make soap out of. I bet that money never made it back to the King's household account.

One day, the boy who helped empty the chamber pots was sick. I was drafted into service. What an awful chore. Emptying someone's pee and poop was not my idea of fun. Could I pretend to be sick, too? Before I could come up with a plan, a man I'd never seen before pulled me by my ear. I suppose he was a substitute, too. Had the whole staff fallen ill?

As I carried the slops to the ditch, I held my breath as long as I could. When I was finished with that chore, I had to get the chamber pots back to their proper owners. The one with the blue flowers went to the Duc, the one with the...what's this? At the bottom of a chamber pot, Benjamin Franklin's face looked up at me. It was fired into the porcelain. I'd seen the famous man's face everywhere—on mugs, on dishes, but in a chamber pot? Who would have thought that the image of the man who'd discovered electricity would end up at the bottom of someone's bottom?

Dr. Franklin was the most famous man in the world, and he was in France.

To win support for the Colonies, Dr. Benjamin Franklin had been in France a long time. Some years ago, the colonists were so mad at the English Parliament that they dumped English tea into Boston harbor. Unfair taxation was one of their grievances. It had started a revolution. After many years of strife, the revolution was coming to an end. The new nation, America, was coming into its own.

I couldn't think any more about it. Someone wanted me to catch a bird that had escaped its cage. It took me the rest of the day. I only caught it because it smacked into a tall window and dropped like a stone. It had swooped so many times around the endless rooms it was tired and didn't hit full force. I put the little troublemaker back in its cage and brought it some fresh water.

Chapter 4

The old aunts seemed to think I was their personal servant. Of all the people I'd seen in Versailles so far, the old aunts were the last people whose servant I wanted to be. They were quarrelsome old biddies. (Pardon me for saying so). The worst of them was Madame Adélaïde. Madame Victoire was fatter, but a bit nicer. Perhaps she never denied herself a sweetmeat. So many of them had turned into flesh, she could hardly get through a door. Sometimes, I had to bump into Madame Victoire to send her on her way.

Crossing the beautiful gardens with a basket of chives, Emilie saw me do my bumper job on Madame Victoire to squeeze her through the outside door and back into the château.

Emilie laughed so hard she dropped her basket. Chives went everywhere. As I knelt to help Emilie gather them I said, "Those Mesdames keep me busy!"

"Be glad you don't have to wait on Madame Sophie, too. She looked around and whispered, "Her nickname since a child was…Grub."

"What? There's another aunt? Spare me."

"She died not long ago of dropsy. I think another aunt is off somewhere being a nun," Emilie said over her shoulder as she headed for the entrance to the kitchen.

I didn't know what dropsy was, but it was lucky for me that it dropped Madame Sophie.

I heard Madame Adélaïde bellow as soon as I entered the château again. "Jacques? Jacques? Where is that boy?"

"Here, Madame." I bowed the required amount. I didn't care if she was one of King Louis the Fifteenth's sisters; her whining was getting tiresome. Anyway, King Louis the Sixteenth was the man in charge now.

I straightened up and awaited the next order. "Bring me some strawberries," Madame Adélaïde barked. She moved closer, staring at me with bulging eyes. Her face reminded me of an overripe persimmon.

"Why must you always smell of onions? Don't you bathe?"

"Certainly. I bathe on occasion, just as everyone else does."

"For you lot, that doesn't mean sufficiently often."

I took that as an affront. I was not part of some amorphous lot of nobodies. And at night, I bathed as often as I could sneak out with a rag and a bar of soap to one of the King's glimmering fountains. I was very careful not to get much soap in the water. I'd be in big trouble if I did that. I was a refined ruffian, if those two characteristics can possibly go together. The trouble was that after I'd scrubbed myself clean, I still had to sleep on a bed of onions.

Madame Adélaïde waddled away. She could get through the doors without a push from me. Later, I had to wander through the vast wing she lived in before I found her and gave her the strawberries Emilie had been kind enough to fetch for me.

For the first time since I'd been at Versailles, I felt the need to leave the château. There was just too much luxury. I could always tell what time it was. Clocks chimed the hours like tiny people playing bells. Tables were polished so brightly the sheen hurt my eyes. Chandeliers sparkled. Light streamed through the windows. Compared to my cottage home, every inch familiar to me, I felt I was now in rooms made of cut diamonds.

Peasant cottages had no windows. And certainly no grand floor. In the dark of night when I was around eight years old, my father went into one of my grandfather's outbuildings and brought out a threadbare Turkey rug that he knew was stored there. When he unrolled it and settled it upon our earth floor, I tripped over its curled edges. It took weeks for me to get used to the feel of the intricate pattern carpeting the familiar dirt beneath my bare feet.

I had never known the time at home. We simply woke up with the sun and went to sleep when it ducked below the horizon. How I longed for that simplicity.

I burst through the same door I had pushed Madame Victoire through and ran as fast as my high-heeled silver brocade shoes would let me. They were too small and not made for running. I already had blisters on my toes. I didn't ask Emilie how she'd managed to get the shoes, but next time I hoped she'd find a donor with larger feet.

When I could run no more, I got my breath and began to count the windows of Versailles. I gave up when I got to two thousand.

Chapter 5

When I was in the *Galarie de Glaces,* I heard a strange voice say, "*Bonsoir,*"

"*Bonjour,*" I answered. Who was this man who dared be in Court without a powdered periwig? Why had he wished me good evening when it should have been good day?

He had scraggly brown hair and a forehead of furrows any farmer would have been proud of plowing. Aside from that, he was probably the oldest man I had ever seen. Then I recognized him. The man from the chamber pot! Like a great wizard, he had coaxed electricity from the skies. I bowed so low I thought my forehead would scrape the polished wood floor. Dr. Franklin touched me under the chin and brought me upright.

"You don't have to do that to me, certainly not when we are the only two people in the room. I'm an American."

"*Bonjour,* "I stammered.

"*Bonjour*," Dr. Franklin replied. "I now realize I wished you good evening instead of good morning. I know better, but I have a great deal on my mind."

"Your French is quite good, Monsieur."

"Spoken with a Philadelphia accent, I fear."

"Philadelphia is where great meetings are held, isn't it?"

"If not for meetings held in Philadelphia, I might not be here. At one Philadelphia meeting, we declared ourselves independent of England, you know."

"Philadelphia is far across the sea?"

"If there is no bad weather, it still takes about a month to sail across it."

"I've never seen the sea."

"Its blue seems to go on forever. Fascinating. I took the ocean's temperature when I crossed it. As one might expect, the deeper the measuring instrument goes, the colder it is. But occasionally, there is a warm current. It merits further study."

"I would like to see the ocean. I'd even like to see Philadelphia."

"Perhaps someday you shall. You're young. Your future lies before you. No telling where you will go."

"I dream of other lands sometimes. You had quite a fight to win yours from the British."

"Ah, yes. When we knew the British were coming to fight us, we decided to hide a great bell. They might have melted it down and made bullets out of it. They damaged the bell tower where it once hung, so we have to repair it before we take the bell from its hiding place beneath the floor of a church."

"I'd like to hear it ring."

"It will ring in freedom soon now, my lad. I'm working on a treaty that may end the American war for all parties. They will sign it in this very room."

Imagining great men seated within it, I looked around the sparkling *Galarie de Glaces*. "The Hall of Mirrors is merely one of the great rooms in this château. There are so many I have yet to find them all."

"You called it the Hall of Mirrors instead of the *Galarie de Glaces*. You speak English?"

"Yes. My father spoke both French and English."

Dr. Franklin studied me as if searching for what lay hidden within me. "You'll go far, my friend."

The great Benjamin Franklin called me his friend!

∽

Chapter 6

I'd been at Versailles three weeks, and I had yet to lay eyes on the King and Queen. Whenever I heard their grand retinue coming, I hid. I didn't even peek through a folding screen. If the King's glance fell upon me, I could be banished in an eye blink. The King's word was law. He could have said, *What are you doing here? Be gone.* Or worse, *Off with your head,* though I don't think King Louis the Fifteenth had ever done that. My knees shook from just thinking about it.

I didn't have a clue what the King looked like. His face was on a French louis, but I'd never seen that grand gold coin.

The King could say, *Bring me some pickled herring,* and pickled herring would be on his plate. Or he could say, *Bring me a hippopotamus,* and one would appear.

The King was in charge of the entire French world, including islands far away, some of Canada—and even the Louisiana territory.

Thanks to the famous Benjamin Franklin, France had recognized America as a nation, no longer colonies belonging to Britain. I remember my father talking about how important that decision was to the Americans.

Though my parents are dead, they speak in my head. I was forgetting the tone of their voices, but what they said bubbles to the surface of my mind and surprises me.

I had to stop thinking. *Here comes the King.* I was closer to heavy curtains than my favorite folding screen, so I ducked behind them. I hoped my brocade shoes poking out beneath would not give me away. *Footfall, footfall, footfall.* The King never walked alone. I suppose those were the ministers who helped him run the government or some of the Counts who liked to curry favor. Or simply a retinue of palace servants whose positions I could never fathom.

At last it grew quiet, and I peeked from behind the curtain. The way seemed clear. I stood in front of the window and looked the direction from which they had come. *Oh, no, here come two more men.* I turned too rapidly and slipped on the highly waxed wood. I put a hand down and pushed back up as fast as I could, almost vaulting behind the curtain. I held my breath as they passed me. I trembled there for a few more minutes. A hand pulled the curtain back, and my heart stopped beating.

"Come out, my boy. No one will eat you."

"Oh, Dr. Franklin. It's you!"

"I saw you fall, said goodbye to the foreign minister, and excused myself. I wanted to show you something."

He unrolled a paper with a beautiful drawing on it.

"This, my friend, is the great seal of the United States of America. The latest rendering, anyway. Notice the bald eagle with the red and white escutcheon, a sort of shield. See how the eagle has a bundle of thirteen arrows? One for every one of our states. The bundle of arrows means the nation will protect itself. Yet the eagle's right talon has an olive branch. It looks toward peace."

"What does the scroll say, Monsieur?"

"*E pluribus unum*, out of many, one."

"It's very grand."

"As it must be, for it will stand for our nation for centuries to come, God willing. If I know America well, more states will fly under our flag, but we will always honor this seal as a symbol of our beginning."

"I want to see your country more than ever now."

"I have a confession to make."

No one had ever said such to me before. "What, Monsieur?"

"I wanted a turkey for the national bird," he winked. "I must be off now. Nice talking to you, son."

"Jacques," I offered.

"It's a pleasure to see you again, Jacques." He gave me a small bow. I nearly fell over from shock.

I watched his back in its plain leather coat as he walked away. Such a strange, wonderful fellow. What must America be like if Dr. Franklin will bow to me?

As he left me, I glimpsed Madame Adélaïde. I turned heel and walked away as fast as I could. I looked back once. She appeared to be gaining on me. How was that possible? She huffed and puffed almost as much as Madame Victoire when she walked. I ducked into a staircase and ran up it as fast as I could. I heard her calling from the bottom of the stairs, "You, Onion Boy..." I turned at a landing, too far out of range to hear her, or so I told myself.

I knew only that I was above the King's apartments. I tiptoed in case the King could hear me below.

Rumble. Clang. Rumble. Clang. What was that noise? Was there another kitchen nearby? I crept closer.

Dogs ears! What's this? The walls felt blisteringly hot when I touched them, and the noise grew louder than ever. I found a doorway and peeked in. What on earth? There was the glow of a huge fire, and a man with tongs was hammering something that glowed red as well.

"Not bad, not bad, if I do say so myself," the man said as he admired what he held at the end of his tongs.

There was something to be learned here, though I didn't know what.

The man banged a little more, then set the item aside. As I walked closer, I tried to peer over the man's shoulder to see what he was working on, but he was too broad and tall. He stepped back and turned around, untying his heavy apron as he did so.

"*Bonjour*," he said.

I was too startled to give my usual bow.

"You must be new here," the man said.

"Yes, Monsieur. Only weeks now."

"You like the foundry, do you?"

"The foundry?"

"Yes. This is a foundry. I make locks here."

"It seems a place of great mystery."

"It seems that way to me sometimes. Here, I'll teach you a few things." He retied his apron, walked to a table and picked up something orange red.

"This is copper," he said. "It's the first metal man used. Because it rests close to the surface of the earth, it wasn't hard to find nor difficult to identify."

"It's a pretty color."

"Yes, but it's a bit soft. That's why man searched for more metals. Or the metals found man. Take iron, for example." He motioned for me to follow him to a big black rock too heavy for him to lift. It looked like a giant hunk of coal.

"Do you know where iron comes from?"

"No, Monsieur."

"Sometimes, it falls from the sky. The Egyptians thought it came from Heaven. We have just discovered it is a meteorite."

"And a meteorite is?

"A rock that plunges to earth from the sky. The Egyptians were partly right. In this *Cycle de Luminaries,* what the English call *The Age of Enlightenment,* we don't think it came from Heaven or is sent by gods. It may be left over from when the moon and earth were made. This fell in the fields of some of my peasants, by the way."

"I bet that scared them."

"It did. Especially when they touched it, and it was hot. I suppose the meteorite traveled so fast it almost burned up."

"Is that possible?"

"I don't know, but the meteorite *was* hot. There were several witnesses."

"I'd like to have seen that landing."

"If you work with metals, you're called a blacksmith," the man said. "Now look at this." He led me to a shiny metal that lay on a table in the corner. "This is the base of what I hope to turn into a lock. It's made of bronze. Mixing copper and tin in the right proportions makes bronze, a stronger metal."

"This *is* a mysterious place."

"You haven't seen anything yet. Here, watch this."

He picked up a big rock and put it on some burning coals. After a while, he pulled the rock from the hot coals with a shovel and dipped it into a bucket of water. *Crack.*

"Come, come." He waved me over. "See? I took ore, which is a mixture of metal and rock, and cracked it by temperature shock. That makes it release its iron."

"And gold?"

"You need a goldsmith to work that precious metal. I have coin and crown makers for that."

No, it couldn't be. This man couldn't be the…

A servant in bright green livery, not faded like mine, appeared and announced, "Sire, your foreign minister would like to speak to you."

"Yes, Yes. All right. Tell him to meet me in the usual receiving room."

"Sire?" I bowed so low my nose hit the floor.

The King took my bow as his due and walked away, untying his heavy apron as he went. I managed to stand again. He turned to me and winked, "This is one place the old aunts won't find me. Come back whenever you can spare time from your duties. You seem like a bright fellow who'll not ask me for anything."

"No, Sire. Nothing."

"That's a relief," he said, grabbing his powdered periwig from a stand near the door. It was only then I noticed that the buckles on his shoes were made of diamonds!

I went back the way I had come. Otherwise, I could have been disoriented in the labyrinth of rooms. When I got back to the place where I had talked to Benjamin Franklin, I heard wailing in the distance.

It is sometimes hard to tell what direction a sound comes from here. Sound bounces like a rubber ball. After a few false starts, I thought I knew which way to go.

"Aaaaaaaaaaaaaa," someone moaned.

"Eeeeeeeeeeeee." There it was again, higher in scale.

"Iiiiiiiiiiiiiiiiiiiiiii." Higher and more desperate in tone.

When I turned the corner, I knew instantly whom the sound was coming from. Madame Victoire.

"Oh, Pet, thank goodness you're here." I suppose being called Pet by Madame Victoire was better than being called Onion Boy by Madame Adélaïde.

"Give me a pull, will you?" she said.

I didn't know where to grab her. She had a bosom the size of two bed pillows, and I didn't think they would make good handles. Her arms were pinioned at her sides, and all she could do was make a small movement with her left hand. I grabbed it and pulled.

"Ooooooooooooooooooooo," she squealed. "You're hurting me!" I dropped her hand.

"Madame, if you'll allow me, I shall push from behind."

"Oh, certainly. I forgot. It's because I'm so mortified to be stuck again. I'm going to have the *bonbonnière* removed from my apartment, so I won't have chocolate morsels or lemon drops at hand." She attempted to turn her head to see where I was going.

I sized up the situation. This was a smaller door than the one that opened to the outside gardens. I didn't think a push would free her, so I stepped back a few yards for a running start.

"Uuuuuuuuuuuu," she said as I knocked the breath out of her. I only tilted her. I waited for her to get her breath and then walked back farther than before. This time I took my shoes off, hoping I could run faster and not slip as I had that day with Dr. Franklin.

Fast. Faster. Fastest. I was almost flying through the room. *Swoosh! Sliding, sliding, sliding,* I slid right under Madame Victoire's hoop skirt and petticoat.

"Pet, get out of there! What if someone sees?"

I fought fabric in every direction, but I couldn't find my way out. It was dark in there. It took so much fabric to cover Madame Victoire's body I felt a ship's canvas had entrapped me. I thrashed around enough to glimpse daylight and crawled desperately toward it.

"Whooooooops," Madame Victoire said. I uplifted her as I crawled through. For a moment, I thought I was a hobbyhorse and she my rider.

"Sorry, Madame. I'll have another go."

"Please do. Oh, I've lost my fan. Wherever did it go?"

"It's probably under your sail…oh, excuse me…I must try another run." My cheeks were hot with shame. I hoped she didn't hear my remark about her sail.

Madame Victoire gave me an imperious look. Clearly, her patience was running thin. Too bad the rest of her wasn't. To make matters worse, the royal ladies wore *paniers*, basket-like things on their hips that made them even wider. I suppose I could go for help, but if she were embarrassed that I'd found her, what would she feel if someone higher up the chain of palace etiquette discovered her plight?

Perhaps if I had something to push with. "Don't give up. I'll be right back."

By the time I ran up to the foundry and down again, I was huffing and puffing almost as much as Madame Adélaide had been.

"Hold on," I gasped.

"Hold on? Hold on? That's exactly what I don't want to do. I'm trapped everywhere but my left hand, and all it can do is flap! Be quick about it."

"Yes, Madame."

I found my shoes, slipped them on and scuffed them across each other for traction. Since my run, they seemed to have grown smaller or my feet larger. Maybe this time I'd stay upright.

I grabbed the wig stand and, thinking I was a knight on horseback with a lance, came hurtling toward the hapless Madame Victoire.

Whoooooomp! She fell on all fours. I helped her up. When she stood, she exhaled, "At last that's over," she said as I handed her the fan.

"Might I suggest rubbing a little grease on the doorway before you attempt to go this route again, Madame?"

"Good idea. Add that to your other duties. Perhaps you could follow me around with a jar of it."

"I'm sorry, Madame, but I am often wanted elsewhere."

"Yes. Yes. I understand. Perhaps I'll ask the King for my own private greaser."

For the first time, I realized that Madame Victoire and the King were related. Repetition must be a family habit. Why say *one* yes when two would do?

I felt as weary as if I'd been in a battle of old, riding out with King Louis the Fourteenth, the great-great-grandfather of the current King. That king loved to go to battle. King Louis the Fourteenth had even melted down his silver throne to help pay for one of his wars. I'm not sure I will ever understand royalty, though this king seems nice enough.

Chapter 7

Ramming Madame Victoire through the door had worn me out. I decided to go to the kitchen for some bread and cheese.

Ow...! Something jumped on my back! To free myself, I almost catapulted the monkey into a wall.

He had on a new little red vest with a name embroidered across it. I brought him around so I could read it. *Singe.* I laughed. *Singe* is French for monkey. I looked around for the spaniels, but they were nowhere in sight.

Singe had his chain on, but the link that held the heavy ball was missing. There was no one about who claimed him. I had always delivered him with the dogs, spaniel under each arm, and the monkey on my shoulder. The old aunts took the spaniels into their laps and turned the monkey over to a servant when they grew tired of him. Perhaps he belonged to the King, as almost everything else did.

"What are you doing here, Singe?" The monkey took his paws and turned my face toward him, staring at me as if my eyelids were walnuts he wanted to crack. "Oh, no, you don't. I'm taking you outside."

He bounced from one of my shoulders to the other, chattering excitedly. I was afraid he would foul my shirt like an untrained puppy. I was glad when he calmed down a little. He plucked his chain from my hand, looked at it studiously, then put it back in my hand and tried to jump to the ground. The chain was too short, so I lowered him the rest of the way. At this point, Singe was leading me rather than I him. I had little choice but to follow.

We walked a long way. My feet were getting sore, but apparently monkey paws could take the cobbles better. Singe led me to an octagonal building with faded paintings of wild animals on its walls. Something growled. Singe leapt from the ground and climbed to the beams above. Where were we?

When my eyes adjusted to the dim interior, I saw a lion! I'd never seen a live one before. I fancied I felt his hot breath as he hastened to eat me. Instead, he closed his great jaws and looked bored. Then I saw he was in a cage and had a dog companion. How odd. The lion wasn't even agitated by the monkey swinging above him. He must have been used to Singe.

The wildest of animals were in cages. Others were in vast pie-slice-shaped enclosures beyond.

A rhinoceros caught my eye. The rhino must have been offloaded from a ship in one of our ports and come by a great wagon to Versailles. What a world I was part of now!

I went from place to place, examining every hoof or paw as closely as I could. I studied the direction an animal's hair grew, the way each animal moved.

The lion had a coat the color of copper.

Then I stood stock-still. What was the creature before me? I'd never seen such a creature in a book. It looked half-zebra, half horse, but its coat was a light brown; the stripes stopped where a saddle on its back would rest. I found a tarnished plaque that said the creature was a quagga, a striped horse. Singe jumped on my shoulder, and then sprang onto the quagga. Singe chattered away, and the quagga looked at him as if he understood each monkey syllable.

"'alo," a voice said.

Could the quagga talk, or had Singe learned to imitate an Englishman?

"'alo. It's just 'ere I am." I saw a boy about my age dragging straw toward the quagga. He wore clothes in need of mending—and washing as well. His curly hair tangled around ears that stuck out a bit too much from his head.

"'ave a chomp, old boy," he said to the quagga as he came forward. "Some animal, ain't 'e?" the boy said to me.

"I've never heard of a quagga."

"Rare, I suppose. None in the street fairs in Paris; I know that."

"Have you been to them?"

"Oh, sure. Me Uncle Bertrand wants me to see if there are animals the King might want for 'is menagerie. This 'ere menagerie is run down, ya see. Not like in the time of the Sun King."

The fact that the menagerie was here at all was amazing to me. The boy took my silence as ignorance. "You know, the Sun King, Louis the Fourteenth? 'is was the greatest reign ever in France. Surely, you know that."

"I know he sparkled like the sun because he had clothes made of diamonds."

"It's a wonder 'e could walk, 'e had so many diamonds sewn on. 'e turned this 'ere 'untin' lodge into the great château of Versailles it is now."

"You sound English. How do you know so much about France?"

"Cuz I live 'ere now. I was a lad in London. French mother, English father. Me uncle runs this place of animals. A few years ago me sister and me ran off with a travelin' animal fair in London. We wuz tired of bein' beaten."

"Your parents beat you?"

"Not them. They've been dead these many years. Was beatin' at the orphanage I was talkin' about."

"What brought you back to France?"

"Me boss sold an ostrich to one of the fair bosses. Part of the deal was that we'd bring it across the Channel. I puked all the way. I wasn't about to cross the Channel again, so I stayed with me uncle 'ere at the King's menagerie."

"How do you like it?"

"Fine. He only beats me on Sundays."

"You're joking."

"Maybe. Maybe not. Wat are you doin' 'ere?"

"I do anything honorable anyone wants me to do. It's how I earn my keep."

His green eyes grew greener. "Anythin' anybody wants ya to do? 'onorable, o'course?"

"Yes."

"Well, then, 'ow about giving me a 'and with the fish oil?"

"You feed the fish oil?"

"What planet did you drop from?"

"I grew up far from sea or Seine. I know very little about fish."

"You're ripe for an educatin' then. Come 'round 'ere."

I hesitated. "'round the back there. I'll let you in. Three enclosures down."

As if he understood the entire conversation, Singe hopped on my shoulder. I held his chain to keep it from bouncing against my chest.

Before I got to the indicated area, I saw the boy lugging a bucket from a storeroom. "Lend a hand 'ere. Maybe we can steady the bucket and keep it from sloshin' me clothes. Watch your fancy pants…"

I let go of Singe's chain to concentrate on the chore. The monkey ambled away, poking through some fallen straw.

"I can't help the way I'm dressed. I work at the château."

"I'll overlook your 'ighness then."

"I'm not related to royalty."

"Bet you have a cousin workin' there, though. It's the way things work around 'ere. Better if your cousin was a queen's lady o'course."

"I do have a cousin, Emilie, who works in the kitchen."

"Your chances for promotion don't look so good then. Watch ya don't get any of this fish oil on your silver slippers. Set it down a mo.…"

He took a large black key from his pocket and unlocked the enclosure. I hesitated, unsure what dangers lurked within.

What waited was the rhinoceros! He turned his great horned face in my direction. I thought I would faint dead away.

"You don't expect me to go in there?" I backed up.

"Sure and it's only a rhino. 'e'll even go up to the bars when the visitors come. Open to the public, we are. The King wants people to know how important 'e is. That 'e can call for strange animals, and his navy will bring 'em. I got news for ya. The navy usually won't. Too small a ship, too grand a captain. Some merchants risk it. Anything for coin."

I quaked at the back of the cage until the boy pulled a rag from the band of his pants and threw it my way.

"Dip it in fish oil and rub it into 'is 'ide. Don't worry, 'e likes it."

Hand trembling, I rubbed fish oil into the rhino's wrinkled hide. The huge animal, breathing, heaved beneath my hand. "Why am I doing this?"

"Maybe it keeps 'im from gettin' a sunburn or 'e needs smartenin' up for the ladies. Your guess. But if I don't do it, me uncle'd drown me in fish oil. Orders from the King, I suppose. Isn't everything?"

"The King can't possibly tell everyone everything that has to be done. He'd be doing nothing else all day."

"Isn't that his role? Telling the French what to do?"

"I suppose. I know he likes to get away from people asking him for things, so it's not all one way."

"You've seen 'im up close?"

"Yes, but not in his royal robes."

"Dresses like a ploughman, this one does. 'e's not a dandy like the Sun King. Oh, those were the days. Did you never hear the stories?"

"A few, I guess. Papa was more interested in stars and planets. He told me more about Galileo and Newton than the Sun King. Did you know the earth goes around the sun and not the sun around the earth?"

"Never thought about it."

The rhino harrumphed and I jumped away, almost upsetting the fish oil bucket.

"Settle. Settle down. 'e won't hurt ya. Rhino's tame. 'e's been 'ere quite a while. Give me your 'and." He led me toward the rhino's head. By the time we were eye-to-eye, my knees were shaking. The boy thrust my hand into the rhino's mouth. *I trusted this boy, and he's feeding me to a rhino!* Instead of eating me, the rhino licked me. His tongue was soft as the velvet pouch hanging on my chest. When my heart slowed down, I took my hand and touched the rhino's horn. It felt like a hairy fingernail. How strange…

I couldn't savor the moment because Singe got jealous—not of my attention to the rhino, but the rhino's attention to me! He jumped on the rhino's back and grabbed its horn, turning the animal toward him and away from me.

My new friend laughed. "Nothin' like true love," he managed to say. "Come on. There's more work to be done." I followed him out of the cage.

Before the great key was put into the lock, Singe shrieked and landed on my shoulder. I wondered if this was one of the locks the King had made. Probably no one would tell stories about this king being a locksmith. It seemed so unlike what a king—who could do anything he wanted—would choose to do.

Singe would not calm down. He was in a bad temper. I couldn't spend any more time with the boy, because Singe pulled me past the quagga's enclosure and led me back to the château the way we had come.

"Name's Jean," the boy shouted after us.

"Jacques," I called over my shoulder.

Chapter 8

I took Singe back to the aunts' apartments and left before they could think of another order for me. I'd learned to be quick around them, especially Aunt Adélaïde.

"Onion Boy," she shouted, but I didn't hear her, did I?

It was close to noon. The kitchen would be humming with activity, but I wanted to find Emilie and finally get the cheese and bread I'd been after before Singe led me away.

Emilie was peeling carrots and slicing them into rounds.

"It's about time you came to see me."

"Did you know about the rhinoceros?"

She waved a carrot at me. "When I can get away, I bring him a carrot."

"He's not a meat-eater?"

"Oh, no!"

"Singe seems to know him."

"Singe knows his way around. He's an impossible snoop."

"I've found the forge and the menagerie. Are there other wonders I should look for?"

"Except for all the rooms decorated with gold, you mean?"

"At first I was dazzled, but now I even walk through the *Galarie de Glaces* without noticing it. This place is so full of surprises that I think I am living in a dream—even if I do have to empty a chamber pot on occasion."

Emilie laughed. "Well, if you can't be a noble, you might as well live among the nobility, though some of them are so haughty you want to…to…stick a carrot up their nose."

"Why, Emilie, I've never heard you talk like that."

"All that glitters is not gold, Jacques."

"You're not happy here?"

"Happy enough, I suppose, though I'd settle for a man I loved and children of my own."

"I guess that's why my father could give up the noble life."

"Begging your pardon, Jacques, but your father had little choice. When he fell in love with your mother, his aristocratic father and mother would have none of it."

"Tell me about it…."

"What a fool I am. As if you didn't know…"

"That's over now. I have to make my own way. At least, I found you." I leaned into her, the closest I could get to a hug in this mass of working humanity. I longed for someone to put their arms around me as Maman and Papa once had.

"Jacques, forgive me, but don't stand so close. You smell of onions." Emilie turned and saw the hurt on my face. "No one has thrown you out of the château yet, so I think you're safe now. Maybe you can find another corner to sleep in."

"I hope so. Every time I see Madame Adélaïde she calls me Onion Boy, and she doesn't care who may be listening."

"That's unkind. I'm sorry I mentioned your odor, but onions make me cry. Just the thought of them makes me tear up. I don't want to lose my job weeping over nothing. Where would I find another?"

I hung my head in understanding. She grabbed my hand. "Tell you what, move the onion bags over by the mushrooms and make a bed of the bags of rice that were just delivered."

I brightened. Perhaps if I smelled like rice instead of onions, Aunt Adélaïde would quit calling me that odious name.

"And please take the flour sacks to the pastry kitchen. They were stacked in our storeroom by mistake. The bakers have been screaming for them since early this morning."

I took to the task right away. The heft of the onion bags strained my shoulders as I dragged them across the floor, but it was better to have them in a far corner than under me. Every morning I'd had their bulbous imprints on my body.

The bags of flour were more awkward to move than the bags of onions. There seemed no way to get a handle on the huge bags. It was like trying to move a feather pillow weighing fifty pounds. Finally, I crawled beneath one and wrapped it around my shoulders. My shoulders were soon covered in white dust.

I hoisted them one at a time to a kitchen area I hadn't been in before. Trusting the scent of baking bread to guide me, I walked hunched over and watched each step of my silver brocade shoes.

"About time," a voice said. "Put it at the back there. No time to put it in the storeroom. We have to make a thousand *petits four* for the dinner tonight, and we're next in the oven line."

I staggered to the back wall and lay down my burden. When I looked up, I realized there was a great flurry of activity. One man was making a cream sauce that smelled of vanilla, another taking loaves of bread from the oven, another…

A man rushed up to me and opened the sack that I had just delivered. "There's always a flour shortage," the man said. "Even for the King. Bring us more. We're running behind on the tarts."

I saw the *petits four* maker glare at the man. I expected a fight to break out between them. As the maker of the *petits four* approached, I turned and ran from the room. Perhaps if I brought another sack of flour quickly enough, I could save some one from getting a black eye.

When I got back, both men were scooping the last of the flour out of the first bag. I laid the new bag down, and both men turned to it as though dogs after fresh meat. One of them took a knife from his apron and cut the bag open in one swift motion.

By the time I delivered the last bag, the *petits four* man was carrying a sheet of white batter to an oven. That must be how the little cakes started out. I'd presumed the dainty little cakes began their life as little squares. Just shows what I knew. Peasants never had any white flour. Only husky brown flour for our daily bread. What we lived on, really. When we didn't have any flour, we were very unhappy—and very hungry.

Of course, we had to use the oven of the estate owner. In this case, my grandfather showed mercy. Peasants had to pay for the use of an oven, but we were allowed to use my grandfather's at no cost. We were even allowed to hunt on his land, something other peasants wouldn't dare do on the land they lived on. Not if they were afraid of getting caught anyway. So my grandfather was not a total ogre.

The people of Paris bought their bread from a bakery. Having your own oven was unheard of. Who could afford to burn wood in such a manner? When I saw the fires around me, I answered my own question. The King.

Chapter 9

That night, I found my bed of rice somewhat more comfortable than onion bags. The brown rice had a distinctive smell, but the bags weren't as lumpy as bags of onions.

When I got up, I wondered if any *petits four* were left from the night before. If I were lucky, there might be one on a platter that someone had forgotten to clean up after the feast. I made my way to the pastry kitchen and found the air white with flour again.

The *petits four* baker and the tart man were talking amicably. The tart man was cutting apples into fine slices. The *petits four* baker was surrounded by pans of batter. He yawned. I suppose he was waiting his turn at the ovens.

They looked up from their conversation when they saw me. "Not so many to bake for today."

"I was wondering if there was anything left over. I'd love a *petit four* for breakfast." Emilie had given me my first one, and I had quite a taste for them now.

The *petits four* man reached beneath a counter and held up a full tray. "Have one on me. You came to our rescue just in time yesterday."

The tart maker patted me on the shoulder. Yesterday's flour, that had settled on my clothes, rose in a cloud. I'd have to shake myself like a wet dog to be rid of it.

Bypassing *petits four* decorated with a pink ribbon of frosting, I took a *petit four* with the same gold symbol I had seen everywhere in the château.

"You fancy the *fleur-de-lis*, I see," the baker said, quite proud of his decoration.

"Is that what it's called? Why are they everywhere here?"

"It's a symbol French kings have used as far back as the twelfth century. Might be based on the iris, though I've yet to see a gold one."

The tart maker chimed in, looking the other baker in the eye. "Do you not believe the legend?"

"That God sent an angel to King Clovis and told him to put the *fleur-de-lis* on his heraldry flag? Who knows? I don't think an angel has appeared to this lumbering Louis."

"I like the King. He's quite nice," I said.

"A friend, is he?" They laughed and pounded each other's back, flour rising above them.

"No, really. I met him in the foundry."

"That alone makes him odd. Imagine a king who can command his whole world choosing to bang about on locks."

"He likes making them."

"I like making *petits four*, too, but if I could command my whole world I'd get someone to bake them and bring them to *me*."

"Wouldn't that get boring after a while?"

"Telling everyone what to do? I'd like to try it for a fortnight. *Bring my crown. Prepare my bath. Bring me a rhinoceros.*"

"There is one, you know."

"There's what?"

"A rhinoceros here."

"I never use the menagerie entrance. Too much bother. I saw a rhinoceros in Paris when I was a boy. That'll hold me for a lifetime, the wrinkled old thing."

"This one is quite tame. I rubbed fish oil into its hide."

The *petits four* baker eyed me closely. "You have time to do that?"

"Once," I said.

"What's your job around here?"

"I do anything honorable anyone asks me to do."

Both men studied me closely. Then the *petits four* baker said, "The next time we're frantic in here, I think we could use you. Come around before then, and we'll teach you a few tricks of the trade. Pick a time when the King isn't throwing a grand feast. We've got to start you out slow and work you up to speed."

"I'd like that. The smell alone makes me hungry."

The *petits four* baker offered me another frosted square. "If you don't see me, ask for Pierre. And he's Henri."

I took a *petit four* with a ribbon on it this time.

"Jacques," I said. "Pleased to meet you."

When I first came I could hardly digest broth, and now I'd worked my stomach up to something too sweet for breakfast and savoring it.

A servant appeared in the doorway and announced, "The Mesdames wish apple tarts sent to their apartments right away. Henri quickly reached beneath the counter and put some apple tarts from a baking pan onto a silver tray. He handed it to me. So I'd have a free hand, I popped the rest of the *petit four* in my mouth.

"Be a good little man and take these to the Mesdames apartments," Pierre said. "Do you know the way?"

"I do." I hurried away.

Wishing I had gone on to Madame Victoire's apartment instead, I hesitated at the door to

Madame Adélaïde's. No matter. Madame Victoire was seated there. Where one aunt was, usually the other was. Madame Adélaïde was playing a Jew's harp while Madame Victoire worked on a tapestry. Needlework was a palace pastime. What else did the royals have to do?

"Onion Boy," Madame Adélaïde said. "About time you showed up around here. Have you been avoiding me?" She came closer, prepared to sniff and make her usual haughty face. But when she got close, she drew back, shocked.

"What's this? You smell…you smell…of *white*."

"I didn't know white had a smell, Madame."

"Neither did I. But you definitely smell of it. What *have* you been doing?"

"Anything anyone asks me to do, Madame."

"Is that so? You haven't done everything I've asked you to do."

"What is that, Madame?"

She scrunched up her face. "I can't recall, but I know I have called you without reply. Are you hard of hearing?"

"I had the pox. No telling what that will do to you."

She made a face and drew closer to mine. Did I see pockmarks on her face as well?

"That was a long time ago," I said.

"Leave me. And take the smell of white with you."

Madame Victoire lumbered after me. She could get through the door to this apartment. She pulled me aside—so that Madame Adélaïde couldn't see us.

"Onion B... Oh, I'm sorry, have you a name?"

"Of course, Madame. Jacques."

She reached inside her muff. "Please take this jar to the kitchen and get some more butter. It works quite well to slip me through most of the doors. There are still some that I haven't braved yet. I don't always know if you're about."

"Yes, Madame."

"Bring it right back. I want to visit the Queen."

When I went into the pastry kitchen, Henri and Pierre were surprised to see me. "Not now, Jacques. We're too tired from yesterday to take on teaching chores," Henri said. He looked quite weary. He was much older than Pierre.

"It's not for me. Madame Victoire wants this jar filled with butter."

"Whatever for? She hasn't ordered any toast."

It took me a while to explain. When I finished, the two bakers were laughing so hard they couldn't have carried a pan to the oven if their lives depended on it.

That night as I slept, it dawned on me that the scent of flour was why Madame Adélaïde thought I smelled of *white*.

Chapter 10

I had a new game. I smelled the sides of every narrow doorway I passed through. If I smelled butter, I knew that Madame Victoire had squeezed through before me. Just thinking about it made me smile. I had yet to reveal to Pierre and Henri that I could follow Madame Victoire's trail if she got lost. I thought about telling Pierre one day, but I didn't want him to laugh so hard he'd fall into the large vat of blackberry jam he was stirring.

I had just walked through a door that didn't smell of butter when a servant woman rushed up to me. "Take this to the *coucher*. Now! Even with all the fires going, it was so damp today I had trouble getting the King's nightshirt dry and ironed. He would pick today to ask for this one."

"Begging your pardon, but what is a *coucher* and where is it?"

"The King's bedroom. Off with you now."

It took me a while to find my way to the King's bedroom, though I had an idea where it was, of course. When I'd first come, I didn't want to go near it. I had feared the King might spot me as out of place and banish me. Now that I knew him, I felt relatively safe, though I still approached with a few ripples of fear.

When I found it, I was aghast. Surrounded by the highest nobles, the King stood naked! I'd heard the fairy tale of the Emperor having no clothes and wondered if I had fallen into it. As I drew closer, I realized the King was wearing some sort of undergarment from the waist down. I couldn't understand why he was standing there shivering. His chest was as white as the underbelly of a fish.

"At last," someone said as he took the folded garment from me. Instead of running forward to drape the cold King in its slightly warm folds, the people merely passed the garment from noble to noble as if it were a breakable treasure. Each man seemed to know his part, but something went amiss. One man changed places with another, and the garment was handed back to the man who had taken it from my hands in the first place. Then it was passed around again, a slow merry-go-round, until it ended up in the hands of the noble standing closest to the King. That man allowed, or helped, the King to put it on.

The man who had taken the garment from me waved me out of the room, and the others followed. I was so confused I went straight to Emilie, who was tidying up her part of the kitchen.

"I've just come from the *coucher*."

Weary, she put the back of her hand on her forehead. "So you've actually seen it?"

"I saw something. I'm not sure if what I saw was a *coucher*. It reminded me of a merry-go-round."

She laughed. "Certainly, there were some horses' backsides there."

That made no sense to me. No painted horses had swirled around the room, only nobles or royals wearing powdered periwigs.

"Maybe you'll be privileged to see a *levee* then."

"What on earth is that?"

"That's when they dress the King and the Queen in the morning."

"They don't dress themselves?" The thought of someone dressing the royals like they were children seemed ridiculous.

"The Duc d'Orléans, the King's cousin, the second richest man in France, has the honor of actually handing the garment to the King. And the King doesn't even like him. The others are important bit players. They must stand in a certain orbit. If they're out of place, they have to start over. Royal etiquette is so formal that even the Queen tires of it."

"I'd be tired of it before it started."

"So is the Queen. She grew up in the Austrian Court, of course, and things were simpler there. That's why she so often stays at the Petit Trianon down the road. She's made herself a haven there. Fewer attendants, less formality."

"I don't blame her. I think I saw her walking in the gardens one day with Madame Marie Thérèse. The child is about five now?"

"Little Madame Royale. Her birth was not the boy the kingdom wished. A girl can't become ruler of France. But the King and Queen cherish her. It took them such a long time to bring a child into the world that France was quite mad at Marie Antoinette. And do you know what? Soon after she gave birth, a ring stolen from her was returned. Her enemies were using it to put a spell on the Queen so that she wouldn't have any children! It must have worked for a while."

"From what I hear, France seldom gives the Queen credit for doing anything right."

Emilie turned away to dry some kitchen silver. "Do you know anything about the *levee* and the *coucher*?"

"Only what I saw."

"It started with the Sun King. As everyone knows, the sun rises, the sun sets. Louis the Fourteenth thought he was as bright and important as the sun and wanted his rising and setting to be a ceremony."

"Louis the Fourteenth again. He haunts this place."

"Haunt is probably not the right word, but his influence is strong. Louis the Fifteenth wasn't that impressive and Louis the Sixteenth is even less majestic. Ah, but Louis the Fourteenth...What a ruler."

Then she whispered, "When he was young, they kept Louis the Fourteenth in such poverty that he had to sleep in ragged nightclothes. He wasn't old enough to rule yet, you see, and there were those who plotted against his ever ruling. We don't talk about the bad times he went through, not in this place, for there followed more grandeur than the world had ever seen. France was the envy of the world."

"Are we still?"

"Teetering a bit now. Louis the Sixteenth hasn't done much to bring us back to our former glory. Trying to upgrade the menagerie seems a rather feeble attempt to impress people. In Louis the Fourteenth's day, the menagerie was so great that he used to entertain heads of state there and put on thrilling animal performances... And..."

Emilie seemed troubled. "And?" I prompted.

She continued, nervously pulling on one eyebrow "He'd sometimes pit different animals against each other to fight to the death. Some of the horrid street fairs still do. There's a painting of such from Louis the Fifteenth's time. A lion being attacked by wild dogs!"

Only a little while ago, I had been happily following a trail of butter. Now I left Emilie with a heavy heart. I wandered over to the menagerie to assure myself that no animal fight-to-the-death was happening there. This time of year, I would have time to make it there and back to my bed of rice before dark.

As I approached, I heard what I thought might be Jean's voice calling. A few more steps and I saw him waving his arms in my direction.

"Come on, I need 'elp 'ere."

I ran as fast as the uncomfortable silver shoes would let me.

"I can't find the quagga," Jean said in a panic. "I went for fresh straw, and I must not 'ave locked 'is gate. I've looked everywhere within the fenced area, and 'e simply isn't there." Jean ran around like a mad man.

"Slow down." What little I knew of animals told me that if you want to catch them, you don't run after them like that. *Whooooosh.* Something ran past me. The *quagga.* I ate my words, for if we were to catch it, we would have to run after it. Otherwise, it could be on its way to Paris by the time we caught up. He might end up in one of the awful animal fights!

"You go that way; I'll go this way," I shouted to Jean. "We'll try to round him up and flush him back into the enclosure."

Singe jumped on my shoulder. Where had he come from? He was not dragging his chain. Only the metal collar remained. Sensing there wasn't enough chain for me to hold, he grabbed my hair with his paws. I didn't want his weight, but I couldn't throw him off unless I wanted bald spots when my hair went with him.

Splashing through the day's rain puddles, the quagga galloped past again. Singe leapt from my shoulder and jumped onto the head of the quagga, chattering and screeching all the while. The quagga slowed, not to a trot, but no longer at its former speed. I looked for Jean. He was too far away to be of help. It was up to me. I used the same running start that I had perfected for Madame Victoire's problem and propelled myself atop the quagga's back. There was little to hold onto. Grasping the quagga's main was like holding onto a hairbrush in a whirlwind in hopes the hairbrush would keep you safe. The main had been neatly trimmed or perhaps grew that way. There was nothing I could do but squeeze my legs around the quagga's belly, bend over close to its head and encircle its neck with my arms. I held on for dear life. To add to my stress, Singe jumped on my head again. We were getting nowhere.

The quagga just kept running around in ever-tighter circles. I felt Singe turn. He twisted himself until he was looking straight into the quagga's left eye. Did the quagga recognize him? Instead of trying to reach the speed of the wind, the quagga slowed. Three or four more lurching laps and he headed toward his enclosure as though ready for a bit of straw and a good night's sleep. I exhaled at last. When I dismounted, my legs shook so much I thought I would fall down. To take my mind off that, I turned to Singe and patted him on the head. It's a good thing Singe and I were acquainted. Otherwise, we might have ended up in Paris!

Chapter 11

Singe and I waited until Jean locked the enclosure, and then, still shaken, we headed back to the château.

The next day, I thought I might wander down to the menagerie and see how Jean had fared with his uncle. I was headed that way when I saw Jean coming toward me.

He seemed to have changed into another boy overnight. He'd even combed his hair. "I wanted to thank ya for your 'elp," he said. "Before me uncle came round, I had time to groom the quagga. The animal didn't 'ave a drop of sweat on 'im when me uncle looked in. I went to me supper without a row. If the quagga had gone missin' I can't bear to think what me punishment would be. If not from me uncle, then from the King."

"The King would understand. He's a kind man."

"Perhaps. But he is also the King, and you should never forget it!"

Unsure what to say, I drew a circle in the mud on the cobbles with the toe of my shoe.

"I didn't come to scold," Jean said. "I've come to invite you to Annonay."

"What's Annonay?"

"You haven't heard?"

"Heard what?" I really didn't know.

"It's where the Montgolfier brothers are going to demonstrate their balloon."

Because I had to ask, I felt ridiculous. "What's a balloon?"

"A marvelous new invention."

"What does it do?"

"It flies!"

"Like a bird?"

"I'm not sure, but 'ere's 'ow it 'appened. On a cold winter's night one of the Montgolfier brothers was watchin' smoke go up 'is chimney. As it did, some laundry dryin' over the fire puffed up. Fascinatin'. Later, 'e took some cloth, stretched it just so, and lit a fire under it. Blimy, if it didn't 'it the ceilin'. That excited him s'more. 'e spent the rest of the winter and spring makin' a balloon. Got 'is paper makin' family to 'elp, and now 'e's goin' to fly it in Annonay."

"No way."

"Yes, way, 'less the stories are wrong 'e's going to have a demonstratin' over to Annonay. I've asked me uncle if ya can ride on the wagon with us. 'e's goin' after a two 'eaded goat."

"It sounds great."

"Can you get away?"

"I don't see why not. I'm not on the payroll, and no one is really my boss."

"Except the King."

"Well, maybe, but he doesn't ask me to do anything. I *am* supposed to come back to the foundry when I can. I'll ask Emilie to find a boy to take out the candle stubs. That's my only regular task."

"It's done then. Be ready day after tomorrow. We'll leave at five in the morning. We've rounded up someone to care for the menagerie while we're away."

"Where shall I meet you?"

He thought for a minute. "At the back of the quagga enclosure. I want to make sure the lock holds."

After we climbed on the wagon that morning, Jean lay on a stack of straw and looked at the gray clouds.

"Imagine bein' up there. It must be like floatin' in a river."

I held out my hand to the breeze. "Floating on a river of wind. I'd like that better than riding a galloping quagga with no saddle."

Jean laughed. He was silent for a moment and then said, "Know why they call it a balloon?

"No clue."

"You 'aven't been in a philosopher's lab, then."

"There aren't too many of those about."

"The King has one of sorts, but mostly he leaves that to the Academy."

"What's that?" This simple boy knew far more than I did.

"Smart men the King appoints to figure 'ow the world works."

"Are the Montgolfier brothers part of the Academy?"

"Nope. They done it on their own."

"I don't see what a laboratory has to do with naming a balloon."

"Come to think of it, that is strange. If the Montgolfiers didn't have a laboratory, how did they know 'bout the round glass vessel called a balloon?"

"A glass vessel?"

"Laboratories are full of glass. All shapes and sizes. They're always putterin' about puttin' fluids and air in 'em. And they tinker with strange machines."

"How do you know?"

"Delivered a guinea pig to the best laboratory in the whole wide world once. It's right there in Paris. Belongs to a man named Antoine Lavoisier."

"I've never been to Paris."

"It's full of wonderful things. Not as decorated with gold as this 'ere place, but it's got some cathedral, I can tell you that. And the Louvre? That's the palace where

King Louis the Fourteenth lived before he moved to Versailles. It's a little run down now."

"Louis the Fourteenth again. Everyone swoons when they speak of him."

"France in her glory."

"Living under Louis the Sixteenth isn't so grand?"

"Ah, no. He's markin' time before the deluge."

"A flood?"

"Not the kind you mean. When old King Louis the Fifteenth was dying of the pox, he said, *After me, the deluge.*"

"I don't get it."

"You're not wise in the way of politics, are ya?"

"Apparently not."

"There are always those out to get the King. Louis the Fifteenth managed to live out his life, but he feared his grandson, this Louis, might not be able to control the people's resentment."

"What resentment?"

"The peasants are full of resentment. Taxes too high on salt and tobacco. Bad wheat harvests. When bread's short, they get fierce with anger."

Remembering my own days of hunger, I understood desperation. I remembered Papa turning his gold ring round and round on his finger. I think he was considering begging some food from his parents.

I was brought back to the present by Jean saying, "For the nobility, their resentment is about control.

They's always wantin' more power, more money, more 'lightenment." Jean practiced, "En-light-en-ment, the English call it. The French have another term, *Cycle de Luminaries,* but it means the same thing. Not believin' in fairy tales no more. Lookin' for truth."

"Can the King do nothing to make the people happier?"

"Oh, he tries, this one. But 'ave you ever seen a king stop bein' like a king?"

I had no answer to that. I'd never seen King Louis the Sixteenth act like a king. Even during the *coucher,* the King had only looked forlorn and cold.

Chapter 12

"How far to Annonay?" I said as the lay of the land started to change around me.

"Long way. We'll be nights on the road." As Jean said this, his bundle of straw took on a life of its own. Jean jumped up. "What in the devil...?" Something jumped on his back, and he screamed.

"It's only Singe," I laughed. I grabbed Singe and swung him onto my shoulders while Jean recovered.

"Should have known, the little bugger." Singe had no collar on, no chain at all. "There's no way he could have gotten loose from the collar. They must be doing a major repair job on his chain," I told Jean.

Jean pushed the straw around until he could lie back again. Singe and I sat up, enjoying the scenery.

"In Annonay, the taste of the water alone is worth the trip," Jean said.

"Flows out of the stone, it does. Clear and clean and tastin' like 'eaven."

I smiled. "I've never tasted Heaven."

"Neither have I, ya twit. I was just dreamin'."

"If Annonay is so far away, I'm glad I wore my own clothes and not the ones I wear in the château. But these sleeves are too short, and my legs stick out farther than when I came."

"Looks a bit silly with the silver brocade shoes on."

"They're all I have."

"Well, take 'em off. Give your toes some breathin' room."

I did. It felt wonderful. Singe got off my shoulders and started playing with my toes, bending them this way and that to see how they worked.

"I'm surprised the King let your uncle go away for so long."

"Wat 'e don't know won't 'urt 'im. The King 'ardly ever goes to the menagerie. So long as no beasts escape and the animals are fed and watered, 'e probably won't miss us. I'm not on the payroll either. I'm lucky me uncle feeds me."

"Your sister didn't want to come?"

"She didn't stay. Went back to England. Doesn't get seasick, that one."

"Your uncle must really want to see a balloon fly."

"Maybe."

"Maybe? You're going on a *maybe*?"

"If Uncle Bertrand heard about the balloon, 'e didn't tell me. We're going after a two-'eaded goat to sell to a street fair."

"Not to fight to the death, surely."

"Not that bad fair. Sellin' it to the fair that likes the quirky animals. A chicken with a claw that looks like a duck's foot, a parrot wat only says, *You're a goner.* That sort of thing. A two-'eaded goat ought to bring good money."

"How do you know that we'll see the balloon?"

"The town has a wall around it. Once we're inside, me uncle is bound to 'ear about the balloon and want to watch. It's not everyday ya can see a balloon fly."

We were going faster, the horses still lively and happy to be on a journey. Was the wind picking up dust and throwing it our way? I wiped my eyes. Something was in the air, graying the sun. I squinted, trying to see what it was.

"The dust will still be there," Jean said as he watched my efforts. "Whatever it is, it's been in the air a while now. Ya ain't noticed, I bet, stuck in the château so much. Bet ya didn't even notice the sunsets."

"What about the sunsets?"

"Sunrise, too. Like a 'and was paintin' 'em from a new palette. Don't know why."

"Maybe Dr. Franklin will know."

"The great wizard who discovered electricity...."

"He wouldn't claim to be a wizard. He would say he was an observer. He told me the temperature changes in the ocean should be studied."

"Water in the ocean's not all the same? When I jump in a river the water feels all the same to me."

"When he crossed the Atlantic, Dr. Franklin found different temperatures at different depths. *Ow, Singe! My toe won't bend all the way to my ankle.*" Singe chattered, scolding me.

Jean went to the front of the wagon and came back with a coil of rope. He found a knife in his uncle's pack and cut off enough rope to tie around Singe's neck and hang down just enough that one of us could hold it.

"Be careful not to yank too hard. We don't want to 'urt the little bugger," Jean said. "Keep an eye out 'e doesn't get the rope tangled in a wheel."

We counted ourselves lucky that Uncle Bertrand was separated from us by a wooden partition. I didn't think he would be pleased to know he had a new passenger.

I took the rope and tied another knot about six inches from the first. The extra knot might keep it from choking Singe. Neither knot would help if the rope got tangled in a turning wheel beneath the wagon.

Chapter 13

That night we slept in the wagon, hiding Singe in the straw until Jean's uncle, sleeping beside us, started to snore. I pulled Singe on top of me for warmth and huddled as close to Jean as I could without inhaling bits of straw. I still had to muffle a few sneezes

Until we came to a deep gorge, the rest of the long journey passed much the same. I held my breath all the way across, fearing the wagon might be blown over the side. When I could finally take my eyes from the gorge, I saw a walled town high above the road. Annonay.

Jean's uncle went right to the home of the two-headed goat. Money changed hands, and he tied the goat to the back of the wagon.

Singe must have smelled the animal because he flailed about under the straw. Both of us had to hold Singe's rope to keep him from escaping. I'm sure Singe wanted to jump on the strange creature's head. I have no idea which head he would have chosen

I had never seen such a thing. The goat could look in opposite directions at once. I thought it might pull itself apart before deciding which way to go. Hitched to the wagon, it had no choice but to follow. The wheels began to turn, and we headed to the center of town.

When we were sure Jean's uncle was concentrating on the road ahead, we let Singe out to see our new companion.

Singe didn't jump on either goat head as I had expected him to do. Instead, he jumped on me and tried to climb atop my head. I'd never seen Singe frightened. He could jump on a galloping quagga without a thought, but now he was shrieking because of a two-headed goat—and about to pull my hair out.

Jean freed me from Singe's death-grip, and we stuck him back under the straw to calm him. It had the same effect as draping a cloth over a birdcage for a quiet night.

The traffic was getting heavier. I was glad not to have Singe's weight on my head. All the coaches, and wagons, and foot traffic seemed to be traveling to a square filled with people. Something large and colorful lay on the ground.

All traffic came to a halt. Jean's uncle turned the wagon into a field and came to check on the goat.

"*Lemonade*," a voice called.

My mouth began to water at the thought of lemonade. People were milling about, looking festive despite their drab clothes. Now and then, I caught a glimpse of brightly colored silks and satins and knew that some nobles and their ladies were present.

When they spotted the goat, people gathered around the wagon, crowding close to get a glimpse of it. Jean's uncle sized up the situation and stepped forward, hand out.

"Have a closer look, pet this Janus of fate. Have your fortune told by a goat. A bargain. Step right up. If the right head looks at you, it's a *yes*. If the left, it's a *no*. Come on, ask away."

Forcing people into line so that they could ask their questions, Jean's uncle started collecting coins. I scrambled into my shoes and joined Jean and his uncle.

"Does Robert love me?" a peasant girl eagerly asked the right goat head. The goat was so nervous that it looked everywhere but at her. She tried again. "Robert. Does he love me?" Both of the goat's heads looked at her.

"I want my money back," she cried.

"Hold on. Try again. The goat's a bit nervous," I said.

"Does Robert want to marry me?" the girl said desperately.

This time, Jean distracted the left head of the goat, and I stood behind the girl with the last of my lunch carrot in my hand. Whiffing the carrot, the right head looked straight at her. "Oh, he does want to marry me." She ran off, happy at last.

As she did, Jean jumped down from the wagon and whispered something to his uncle. His uncle looked shocked, then nodded. Jean untied Singe from beneath the straw and put him into play. "Come see the monkey. Shake 'ands, 'e will."

It worked well. People paid first for the goat and then the monkey. Twice the coins! It was easy. With Singe secured by the rope in Jean's hand, all anyone had to do was take the monkey's paw and they'd shaken hands with a monkey. Knowing that I could get one of the heads to look at me as I stood behind a waiting customer, I stayed where I was, waving the carrot as needed.

We were doing quite well until a cry went up. "It's begun. They're starting to fill the balloon. Come on, we don't want to miss it." Our customers disappeared as rapidly as they'd come.

I never got any lemonade.

We left the goat tied to the wagon, but Singe leapt to my shoulder, held onto my hair and wouldn't let go. "All right, you rascal. Come along. I won't leave you behind."

We followed as closely to Jean's Uncle Bertrand as we could. I didn't want to get lost in the jostling crowd. As we drew nearer, I saw something bouncing up and down above the heads of the crowd. Blue and gold. It seemed brighter than the sun. We pushed forward. As we did, Singe set up such a clatter I thought everyone would turn to look, but all eyes were fixed on the object bouncing before us. Finally, I saw the entire balloon. It was still tethered to the ground as its massive sides filled with heated air from burning straw. Anxious to be free, the balloon pulled against its ropes.

The weight from my shoulder vanished. "*Singe! Come back*," I yelled. Of course, he didn't. I chased him as far as I could in my frightful silver shoes. He was climbing one of the ropes of the lunging balloon before I could catch him.

Jean saw him. Farther ahead than I was, Jean chased him, too. Singe swung from tether rope to tether rope like a trapeze artist. Up, down, bouncing when the balloon did. The crowd saw the spectacle and started yelling.

The man who seemed to be in charge of the balloon shouted something to Jean that I couldn't hear. Then people surrounded the balloon, and the scene was lost to me.

The balloon took off! The wind held it and then carried it away. *Where, oh where, was Singe?* My heart hammered in my chest. Was Singe clinging to the ropes, too scared to swing back and forth on them now? When the balloon passed over my head, my heart sank.

I heard a familiar laugh and turned around to see Jean, Singe on his shoulder. I nearly fainted.

"At the last possible moment, I got the little bugger," Jean laughed. "Otherwise 'e'd 'ave been clingin' to not much at all, just a valve of some kind at the bottom of the bouncin' balloon. Ain't it grand?" I forgot Singe and watched the balloon. Flight! Into the clouds! Traveling the speed of the wind!

On the way back to Versailles, I lay on the wagon floor, Singe sleeping on my chest. Not only had we witnessed history, Singe had nearly been part of it.

I was in no hurry to get back to Versailles.

༄

Chapter 14

Back at Versailles, I found that everyone knew of the flight of the balloon. Naturally. If something important happened in his kingdom, the King would surely know it. The balloon had flown for ten minutes!

As I dropped off to sleep that night, the balloon still soared in my mind.

The next afternoon, after I had a bowl of lentil soup provided by Emilie, I wandered to the baking area in hopes there was a leftover *petit four*.

Pierre was the first to see me. "Did you hear?" he said. "About the balloon?"

I wanted to say, "I saw it. I saw it fly." I kept silent, not wanting to give away my absence to anyone other than the lad who'd done my chore. And I hadn't told *him* why I wouldn't be gathering candle stubs.

Head down, I said, "It must be a wonderful thing."

"You seem a bit disheartened. Maybe it's time you learned the pleasure of baking. We're not very busy today."

My education as a French baker began.

I learned that butter had a lot more uses than grease for Madame Victoire.

Butter creamed with sugar went into a cake. Butter beaten into frosting dressed up the *petits four*. Butter cut into flour made the crust of a tart. Butter married with yeast and flour rose into bread. Even butter melted in a sauce to pour over a pudding was a delight.

In the weeks that followed, I used butter in all these things. Once, I was even allowed to carry a tray of tarts to the huge oven. They had yet to let me frost the delicate *petits four*, but that would come, I was certain. One day I would learn how to tie a pink frosting ribbon atop its white sides. Doing anything honorable anyone asked me to do was a wonderful thing. At first I had done it for mere survival, but I found it led to knowledge—and knowledge was my weapon of choice.

One day in September, the château was filled with excitement. The Montgolfier brothers were going to have another demonstration. This time here in Versailles! They were going to attach a basket to the balloon and put a sheep, a duck, and a rooster into it. If animals could live in the height and wind of the sky, would they try to send a living, breathing, man into the unknown?

When I walked into the bakery at my usual time, Pierre grabbed me.

"Good thing we've got you trained. It's full out today. Lots of grand nobles are coming to see the balloon go up. Everyone who is anyone is staying here in Versailles as well. And, of course, the King and Queen will be at the front of the crowd. We must turn all our flour into wonderful things to eat. Come on, start mixing." He pointed to a bowl. I took the wooden spoon and found the spoon felt at home in my hand as I creamed the butter into the sugar. I was *really* catching on. Maybe one day I could make a living as a *boulanger.* Will wonders never cease?

∽

Chapter 15

I saw Dr. Franklin in the crowd of onlookers. He wore his buckskin jacket, still unashamed of his straggly hair amid all the powdered heads. The great Franklin waved to me, not caring that I wasn't anyone of importance.

No wonder he was smiling. The King had planned this event to celebrate the signing of the peace treaty that ended the American war. Dr. Franklin had been successful on the quest he had been pursuing the day I met him.

I had thought my first balloon launch exciting, but the expectant air amid the satin clad onlookers here took my breath away. Hoping for a good view, I felt my heart beat faster as I made my way through the crowd.

There the balloon was, still flat upon the ground, its blue sides reflecting the color of the sky, the basket as startling as if it were a giant yellow pillow. Not far away—yes, it must be, Queen Marie Antoinette! She seemed to float across the lawn, she moved so gracefully. I had never seen the Queen up close. My breath caught in my throat.

She had the pout of the Habsburg bottom lip that marked that royal line for generations. Her long nose fought for attention, but her lips won. Then the Queen smiled, and my opinion of her petulant lips was turned upside down. Suddenly, she seemed elegant.

The Queen had abandoned her silk gowns and elaborate hairdos for a muslin dress and a floppy straw hat. I wondered if the quagga or the rhino would like to eat it. After all, wasn't straw, straw? It seemed an odd choice for a woman who could have anything she desired.

I'd heard the King was unhappy about the Queen's choice of dress. He feared the silk industry would suffer. As I looked around, I could see he might have cause to worry. Scattered among the colored satin gowns were many plain muslin ones. They were lighter and less burdensome than the old style, but they seemed to cry, *Look at me. I am like the Queen.*

I turned my attention to the Queen and saw a small boy following her. It must be the Dauphin. He was the future of France. One day it was assumed he would be King.

A man in a drab gray coat was in charge of the balloon. A Montgolfier brother? My eyes followed his gaze as another man lit straw to fill the balloon with hot air. It wasn't long before the balloon began to pull at its mooring ropes, bucking like a horse. It was decorated with gold *fleurs-de-lis*.

The fire was dying down. Someone threw on old shoes, more straw, and foul smelling meat. The stench and smoke forced the King and Queen away. I ran with the crowd as anxious to get away from the stench as anyone else.

Amid the confusion, some brave soul, probably holding his nose, managed to load the duck, the rooster, and the sheep into the basket. The duck flapped its wings frantically, obviously frightened. But then I saw what it was frightened of. Singe! Oh, no! I ran as fast as my silver shoes would let me. No matter where I reached for him, Singe eluded me. I finally had to climb into the basket to tackle him. Something jabbed my ribs. Jean's elbow. He'd seen Singe, too, and both of us were trying to hold Singe down.

"Hurry! We have to get out of here before someone sees us," I gasped.

I swung my leg over the side, but there was no ground to put my shoe upon! I watched in horrid fascination as the land receded from view.

Jean pulled me back in and put his hand atop my head. "'unker down. It's too late now!" We ducked the sheep's nervous hooves and held on to Singe for dear life as he clung to the mooring rope. The duck flapped its wings again and looked warily at Singe. We ignored the duck and hauled Singe aboard just as the wind suddenly swept us higher.

As the wind rushed by us, we lifted our heads, keeping our eyes just above the rim of the basket. The land was so far below us it looked like a crazy quilt. Already in the distance, Versailles looked as if it were a picture in a book of fairy tales. We were over fields dotted with an occasional peasant cottage. Surely, this was the fastest way to travel. My breath caught in my throat. Could it be? Was that my cottage off in the distance? I leaned forward, hoping to catch another glimpse of it, but we flew into a cloud. We *flew* into a cloud.

"We're flying. We're flying," Jean yelled. "The first boys in the sky...*Whoopee...'ooray!*" He stood up. The basket swayed, threatened to tip over! I grabbed Jean and settled him back down. Realizing the danger he had put us in, he didn't move.

Free to concentrate on the wonder of flight again, I smiled so wide I thought my cheeks would crack and break in the cold wind. Then I thought, *Will we live through this?* There had been much speculation about sending men into the sky. So far the King had been unwilling to risk a man's life. First, the King wanted to see if animals could survive. If he only knew...

I watched the duck for any sign that it was struggling to breathe, but the wind ruffled its feathers so much I couldn't tell. Though it wasn't daybreak, the rooster crowed and flew to the rim of the basket. Singe lunged for the rooster. Jean and I wrestled it away from him.

I let out a sigh of relief. If the rooster could crow, it was breathing. How odd that I was watching the animals. All I had to do was know that *I* was breathing. It showed how excited I was. It's not every day two boys get to be the first humans to fly!

My eyes felt gritty. The strange dust I'd been aware of for weeks was blowing even here. I looked up. I was still *in* a cloud. I felt like I *was* a cloud. I *was* the wind. I was...*flying!*

Chapter 16

Eventually, the pull of gravity won over wind and sky. We started our slow drift downward.

Jean and I looked at each other with awe. "Wat just 'appened to us?" Jean said.

"Did we dream it?" I pinched my ankle to see if I felt it. *Yes*. This must be real. I made out the form of a cow in the distance. "We've got to get out of here before we're discovered. We could both lose out jobs over this."

"If you call wat we do a job," Jean scoffed. But he put Singe inside his shirt and prepared to abandon the airship. The thump as we landed was rougher than I expected. The next day, Jean and I both had bruises from the jolt of our tumble. We didn't give the animals another thought. If we were alive, so must they be.

It was a long walk back to Versailles. After traveling at the speed of the wind, walking back was drudgery. I finally took off my shoes and walked barefoot, cutting my feet on an occasional stone. We tired of taking turns carrying Singe and set him loose to trail after us. The little troublemaker!

When we got back to Versailles, the crowd was dispersing. People said the balloon had only flown for eight minutes. A small tear had ripped open.

People were leaving in grand sedan chairs or fancy coaches. Others were lucky enough to be invited to dine with the King and Queen and spend the night. I saw Dr. Franklin heading for the château and caught up with him.

"*Bonjour*," I said, out of breath.

"Jacques. Wasn't it a grand sight? A wonderful way to celebrate America no longer under the yoke of the British. And France is at peace once more with England!"

"Absolutely wonderful," I sighed, remembering.

"Someday man will soar in those clouds."

"I'm sure men will fly!" Glowing with my wonderful secret, I was one big smile inside. But I didn't dare tell him. Besides, I'd caught up to Dr. Franklin for another reason. "Do you know what is causing the strange dust in the air?"

"This dry fog? I think it comes from a volcanic eruption somewhere. Not in France. If it had happened here, we would have heard about it. No, some place far away. Iceland, maybe. That place has many such volcanoes. The dust has lingered quite a while. I fear it is blotting out some of the sunlight and affecting the crops. That does not bode well for France. Hungry people are desperate people."

Remembering my father twisting his gold ring when our food stocks were gone, I understood only too well. But my father was a gentleman. I'd seen wild-eyed peasants, and the thought of their desperation sent a chill up my spine.

I looked up at the sky wishing that the dry fog would dissipate—and soon.

◇

Chapter 17

It was not long before an ambitious noble, Pilâtre de Rozier, convinced the King to send men into the sky—he being one of them, of course.

I was unable to see the flight. The King had me working in the foundry now, and anyway I had no way to get to the Château de la Muette where the balloon was to be launched. The royals had fled to Muette during the last pox outbreak and still liked to spend time there.

Pounding away at the glowing metal that would one day be a lock, I tried not to think about what I was missing.

I suppose this skill might serve me well in the future, but I preferred the smell of the bakery and the heat from those ovens. The hot blast of the foundry furnace almost blew me away. But I wanted to please the King. And I *was* getting better, learning to judge when a metal became more malleable and should be removed from the fire. When I did it right, the King patted me on the shoulder.

There was another reason I preferred the bakery. The King's locksmith. I came upon the King and the locksmith when he was helping the King make a key fit a lock. When I came in, the locksmith looked at me as if I were a rat scurrying across the floor. I turned heel and went rapidly down the hall.

I kept on hammering when I heard Pilâtre de Rozier and the Marquis d'Arlandes landed alive. A great cheer went up when Versailles got the news.

I already knew men could live in the sky, but I couldn't ignore the laughter that followed. What was so funny?

I laid my work aside and stuck my head out the door. "What's going on?" I asked a passing page. He was wearing the Queen's vivid red clothing, her choice of livery. He tried to keep a straight face, but couldn't. I hoped he wasn't noticing my livery, so faded that I was unsure what color it was. With my heavy apron on, maybe he wouldn't see enough of my clothing to make fun of it.

I felt better as the page laughed again and said, "When the aeronauts landed, the peasants were so afraid of the balloon's hissing and huffing, they attacked it with pitchforks."

Now *I* laughed. I'd been in such a hurry to exit the balloon I hadn't noticed the noise of its escaping air. When the balloon collapsed around us, I was too busy walking on something that felt like wriggling bed pillows.

Unfortunately, the aunts would still spy me walking about and send me on errands. They were such gossips! Once they made me stand by them until they finished their conversation about how the Queen's choice of muslin dresses made her look like she was walking around in her chemise.

"And did you see her leading her lambs around by ribbons that matched the ribbons on her dress? Scandalous. What is this Court coming to?" Madame Adelaide said.

I cleared my throat on purpose. She waved in my direction. "Off with you. I changed my mind. We don't need anything."

Bewildered, I left the room. Then it dawned on me. Madame Adélaïde wanted me to hear her defame the Queen in the hope I would spread it among the staff. Well, I wouldn't. What harm were matching ribbons? And I certainly didn't know what the Queen's undergarments looked like, so how could I compare her muslin dress to her chemise?

I supposed I would have to stand there again while the aunts trashed the Queen's hamlet, her special village down the road from the château. She entertained her friends there. Sometimes she even set the clocks up so that the King would return to the château early. Then she and her friends could play on. I didn't need the aunts to fill me with gossip. There was enough already. I'd never known there were so many bad names to call a woman, much less a queen.

Since a man named Beaumarchais, an undercover agent for the Americans, was no longer concerned about raising money for the American Revolution, he'd finished his play, *The Marriage of Figaro*. France and all of Europe, I'd heard, were talking of nothing else. The Figaro character offended the nobility, especially these two lines: *What did you ever do to deserve so much? You gave yourself the trouble to be born and that is all.*

Whoa! The nobility guarded their privileges like peasants guarded bread. Any word that the nobility didn't deserve their hunting and fishing rights, their largely tax-free status, their right to wear a sword, and you started a firestorm. Oh, my!

To make matters worse, Queen Marie Antoinette decided to keep on decorating and building. She was revamping the Saint Cloud estate that she'd bought from the powerful Duc d'Orléans.

Now in the halls I heard whispers, *By order of the Queen*, rather than *By order of the King*. Such a thing was not done. The King was the one who gave orders here. Certainly not the Austrian born Queen.

In the past, the queens of France did not have a personal livery. Yet she did. They didn't walk around with lambs on satin ribbons. Yet she did. They didn't play whist until the wee hours of the morning while the King snored in his empty bed. Yet she did.

A queen who flaunted her wealth was resented, resented, resented. For her own sake, I wished our queen would be more sensitive to what the people of the kingdom thought about her. I was having trouble finding words to defend her against the gossip that swirled in her wake.

Where could I go where I wouldn't hear any gossip? The menagerie, though I expected Jean wouldn't hold back if he'd heard anything interesting. The animals wouldn't talk, thank goodness. They had their own way of communicating.

I didn't leave the château until it was almost dark. The sunset was gorgeous. The dry fog in the air made my eyes sting. They were already irritated from the heat of the foundry furnace. But I saw what Jean meant about the glorious colors of the sunset.

I went to the quagga enclosure. Jean was nowhere about. The quagga seemed to remember me from the time I'd ridden on its back. Singe had calmed the quagga, but I think I helped by hanging on to the quagga during the wild ride.

Approaching the quagga slowly, I offered an apple that I had gotten from Emilie. The quagga quivered for a moment, then parted its lips and took the apple into its wide mouth. I let him enjoy the sensation for a moment, then put my hand gently on its head. It didn't move. I lowered my head to his. The warmth of it and its animal smell soothed me.

So much had happened to me. My parents' death, my journey here, being at everyone's beck and call, learning new trades… It seemed I was everywhere and nowhere. I longed for Maman's touch, my Papa's voice.

Emilie and Jean were my only friends. Though I worked in a place of such grandeur that others would envy my lowly position, life looked bleak.

I finally let go of the quagga's neck and headed toward my bed of rice. I had only gone about twenty steps when it dawned on me that I might have other friends. Dr. Franklin and—*the King*.

I looked at the sky and the faint sprinkling of stars. Because Dr. Franklin had brought electricity down from the sky and helped bring about a new nation, he was the most famous man in the world. The King had most of France at his feet—with the possible exception of the Queen. Yet they both took an interest in me.

By the time I opened the door to the storeroom, I felt better. I lay down on my bed of rice and fell immediately asleep. I dreamed that Pierre and Henri were busy baking and teaching me to make a plum pudding. In sleep, I realized I was not so alone after all.

Chapter 18

When I awoke the next morning, I was ready for whatever the day would bring. I even looked forward to the evening when I would gather the candle stubs. There is comfort in routine

The King wasn't having such a good day. He was struggling with the finances of France. It's pretty bad when a kingdom is running out of money. Aside from the fact that the King spent too much, France had lent so much money to America in its struggle for independence that it made our situation worse. I knew what it was like to be short of money, so my heart went out to the King.

The only good news I'd heard so far this day was that Thomas Jefferson, the new ambassador from America, was coming to join Dr. Franklin and John Adams. Mr. Jefferson had written America's Declaration of Independence.

I'd never met John Adams, another great American, but I saw him looking rather cross as he walked toward a carriage, his wig askew. One day, I spotted him walking in the Queen's garden by Dr. Franklin's side. They were arguing. The wind bore Adams words straight to me. *The trouble with you, Franklin, is that you like the French too much.*

Like us too much? Why not? We were regarded as the most cultured people in the world. We loved opera, the theatre, had grand libraries, dressed well, prepared wonderful food. What's not to love?

I had to admit that only the rich and powerful could lead such lives. In the lives of the poor, life was a constant struggle. Maybe Thomas Jefferson would bring money to repay France. Then perhaps the King would have enough funds to ease the tax burden on his subjects.

∽

Chapter 19

March, 1785, the Queen gave birth to another son, Louis Charles, the Duke of Normandy. What the English refer to as *an heir and a spare*. His brother, the Dauphin Louis Joseph was quite frail, almost constantly running a fever. If he were to die, this new babe would become the Dauphin.

Pretending to dust the library shelves, I took down a volume of Diderot's *Encyclopedia* from the King's library to read about the Dauphins of France. I assumed that the title Dauphin bore a relationship to the sea creatures that signal each other with squeaks. I was right. Such dolphins were on the Coat of Arms of the Dauphin illustrated in the *Encyclopedia*. It came from the Old French *dalfin* and was the title of lords of the Dauphiné.

There was more, but it was kingly politics, and I didn't care about that. I had to go to a newer edition to find out about the current Dauphin.

For a long time, the Queen had borne no children. France desperately needed an heir to the throne. Finally, Queen Marie Antoinette had Maria Teresa, but France needed a boy. No girl could rule.

The Queen gave birth to Louis Joseph in October of 1781. I remember celebrating his birth with my mother and father. That made him special to me. The few glimpses I had of him worried me. He looked so sickly. If we were ever to meet, I hoped I would not need to address him by his full name. I would never get *Dauphin Louis Joseph Xavier Francois* out of my mouth.

Rain. I never thought I would be so wild for it. To want to stick out my tongue and feel a raindrop upon it. All that spring, we roasted. The women at Court no longer bothered to use their fans in flirtatious ways, simply fanning to cool down. If it had been socially acceptable to strip off our clothes and run naked through the gardens of Versailles, we would have.

Hoping for a breeze, I was walking in one of the gardens when I saw Dr. Franklin approaching. He looked like he was heading straight for me. Because his gout was bothering him again, I quickened my steps to meet him. He was quite crippled by it lately.

"Jacques. I was hoping I would see you. My work is done here. It won't be long before I will be leaving for America."

I was stunned. Dr. Franklin had been so much a part of my life at Versailles that I never thought there would be a time when he would no longer be here.

"Don't look like that, my boy. I have fond memories of our time together. Maybe one day you'll visit me in Philadelphia."

"Where the great bell is."

"Remember I told you that we had to hide it under the floorboards of a church when the British occupied Philadelphia so they wouldn't melt it down to make bullets? America is rebuilding the steeple so we can hang it and hear it toll again."

I helped him ease his body onto a wrought iron bench. It didn't offer him much comfort. Pain showed in his face as he talked.

"I'd love to show you around Philadelphia. I'll not be crossing the sea to France again, I'll wager, but you're young. Who knows where you'll go in your lifetime?"

༄

Chapter 20

Bad news. Pilâtre de Rozier and a man named Romain died attempting to cross the English Channel in one of the new balloons. I didn't know if it had been filled with the newly named hydrogen gas or whether it had been fueled by hot air.

Antoine Lavoisier named hydrogen in the very lab where Jean had delivered the guinea pig. Lavoisier also named something present in the air we breathe. *Oxygen.* Would there be no end to what such learned men would discover?

When I stopped thinking about hydrogen and oxygen, I went back to thinking about the disaster. The balloon caught fire off the coast of France. I was sad. But I was relieved that Singe hadn't chosen that flight to give us a merry chase into the clouds.

Perhaps someday, aeronauts would be called pilots in Pilâtre de Rozier's honor.

I hadn't seen Jean for a long time. The King in the foundry and the bakers in the bakery had kept me quite busy. Sometimes, I even ran late to collect the candle stubs. That night, I didn't take the time to turn the contents of my sack over to the servant who took the spent candles from me.

I walked as fast as I could toward the menagerie. The candle stubs thumping against my legs bothered me, so I hid the sack under some bushes and rushed on.

Jean was just closing the door to the rhino's cage after having oiled its hide. I wondered if this was a nightly chore. Surely not. But if the King had ordered it...

"Blimy, let's get out of 'ere. If I 'aul another forkful of straw, I think I'll be as lunatic as the laughin' 'yena."

"I think that's just the hyena's nature."

"Well, it ain't mine. That shows 'ow close I am to runnin' away."

"Your uncle. Has he...?"

"No more than usual. It's 'arder to catch me. I'm growing bigger."

I studied him in the dim light and found he *had* grown. I'd grown since the last time I'd seen him, too. Emilie had to find larger clothes for me several times.

I remember the moment she presented me with the ones I was now wearing. "Lucky you. The washerwoman didn't know how to use this new thing called *bleach* and put it in with the Queen's livery. Bleached the red to pink. After she discarded the livery, I put it in more bleach, rinsed it, and then dyed it in water and lime rinds. Makes it look as if it were the King's green livery. Unfortunately for you, still a bit faded."

On my feet were faded shoes. I didn't ask Emilie if she'd had to bleach those, too. The shoes were actually too large for me. Maybe she had begged them of the redheaded Lafayette, the French hero of the American Revolution. He was the tallest man I'd seen at Court. Without him, the Americans would never have broken free of the British. Lafayette had furnished a ship, fought for George Washington, bought, *yes, shoes,* for the bare feet of some of Washington's troops. I convinced myself that I was walking in Lafayette's shoes

Jean brought me back to the present. "Do you want to come with me?"

"Where?"

"Run away."

"Where would we run? How would we eat?"

"I could steal some bread occasionally."

"No! I would never…"

"Just kiddin'," Jean said, looking down. I wasn't sure. I knew what desperate men could do. Desperate boys were something of an unknown to me. I was the only desperate boy I had known. I thought that I had acted honorably—except when I didn't *hear* the old aunts shouting at me.

"Let's get away from the menagerie. Me uncle might find me. Maybe if I come back late enough, 'e'll be snorin' on the job." We set out as fast as we could.

"I came a circuitous route because I hadn't turned over the candle stubs. I stashed them under some lilac bushes."

"Ya could sell the stubs, ya know."

"I would never…"

"I'll wager someone does and puts the funds in 'is own pocket 'stead of the King's 'ousehold account. The King wouldn't miss that little bit. 'e's too worried about the big debts coming down on 'is 'ead."

"Emilie has heard rumors that some of the kitchen staff will be let go. Not just a dozen or so. Hundreds."

"The King doesn't need so many servers, for sure. I 'ear that Mr. Jefferson went to a dinner where there were three servants to every person. I bet the King 'as ten servers to every guest and about fifty for 'im and the Queen alone."

"That protocol is about as silly as the *levee* and the *coucher.*"

"I can dress me own self. And 'e's sure no Louis the Fourteenth."

"No, but I bet he's nicer. He's been very good to me personally, instructing me in the making of locks."

"So that's wat's been keepin' you away."

"That and working in the kitchen. They're going to let me make all the cherry tarts in a month or so."

"A swell, ya are. Pretty soon ya'll forget ya know the likes of me."

"Not at all. You and Singe and I have had wonderful adventures."

"I 'aven't seen Singe. Where is the little bugger?"

"They've kept him caged. Apparently, they can't keep him under control. We, of all people, should know that."

"Shh! What's that? 'ide in case it's me uncle."

We dove behind a statue. Jean let out a sigh of relief. "It's only Cardinal Rohan. What's 'e doing skulking around in the dark?"

"Hush! Someone else is coming."

A woman appeared.

"Your Majesty," the Cardinal said.

The Queen didn't act queenly.

The couple whispered conspiratorially. The Queen walked about as if thinking, then turned and handed the Cardinal the rose she was carrying. I hissed into Jean's ear, "That's not the Queen. I can tell by the way she moves. And why the rose?"

"Granting forgiveness, I think. The Queen's been mad at the Cardinal for years, but I don't know why." Jean raised his head. The woman turned toward us, her back to the Cardinal, and moonlight fell full upon her face. "It ain't the Queen. Not 'ardly. 'tis the Comtesse de Lamotte-Valois!"

"Never heard of her. Never seen her."

"'ush. They've quit talkin'."

The Cardinal handed her Majesty, who was *not* her Majesty, a small package. She nodded and walked rapidly away, clutching the package to her bosom. The Cardinal watched her depart and then headed back the way he had come.

Tired of hunkering down, Jean and I slid into a sitting position, our backs against the statue's base.

"What was that all about?" I asked.

"The Comtesse de Lamotte-Valois passes 'erself off as a descendant of a prince, but she stays in a low rent room not far from where me uncle and I bed down. She's a sly one, she is."

I was so puzzled by the strange happening that I forgot to speak to Jean of the disastrous balloon flight of Pilâtre de Rozier. I left him and set off to retrieve my stashed candles.

I was so preoccupied that I wandered into a part of the château I had not been in before. The King's funds must be low indeed if he let rooms in the palace get so run down. I was shocked by how shabby they were.

༄

Chapter 21

I was admiring my cherry tarts, still warm from the oven, when I overheard Pierre and Henri discussing a diamond necklace.

"The Queen says she never bought the necklace. Had in fact told the jeweler Boehmer numerous times that she didn't want or need any more diamonds."

"So she says," Henri said gruffly.

"The King backs her up. The King had even refused to buy the necklace when Boehmer offered it to *him* at a discount."

"Another scandal. Just what we need."

Measuring the sugar for vanilla sauce, I thought no more about the necklace.

A week or so later, Jean was waiting by the kitchen door when I came out.

"How long have you been here?" I asked.

"Not long. I've only got a mo'. I 'ave to check on the animals. But I wanted to tell ya. That night? When we 'id behind the statue?"

"Yes?"

"The Cardinal handed the Comtesse a diamond necklace. That's what was in the box."

"And?"

"Don't you get it? 'e thought she was the Queen. Thought 'e was delivering it to 'er. That the Queen 'erself was buying it."

"But why? The King gets her anything she wants."

"Uh huh, but *the people*, think what *the people* would say if the King bought her more diamonds."

"Of course! The people think the Queen spends far too much."

"And get this. The Queen says she'd rather buy more land adjoining 'er St. Cloud estate than more diamonds. Either way, she's in trouble."

"Has she?"

"Wat?"

"Bought more land."

"Don't know."

"But we know it wasn't the Queen who took the necklace."

"Who'll believe the likes of us?" With that, he turned and walked away.

I went on to the foundry where I found the King staring into the fire, no hammer in hand. I put on my apron and went to work the way he had shown me. He never turned or acknowledged my presence. I knew I would not get a pat on the shoulder or a *well done* from him that day.

Chapter 22

Soon, the night of the strange rendezvous between the Cardinal and the supposed Queen became known as the *Diamond Necklace Affair.* The Queen suffered greatly from all the wicked rumors swirling around her. The scandal had gone on for months. To make matters worse, one of the aunt's was on the Comtesse's side. One, perhaps both aunts, dripped poison into the King's ear about Queen Marie Antoinette.

In the end, the Cardinal, being a cardinal, was acquitted of any wrong. He defended himself by saying he'd been tricked. The Comtesse was imprisoned and soon escaped. The rumor was that the diamonds were removed from the necklace and sold. I'll bet the money from the sale of those loose diamonds made its way into the Comtesse's hands.

I was relieved it was over. During that awful time, whenever I saw the Queen, I wanted to run to her and tell her that I knew the truth. Or blurt the truth out to the King. I didn't. I was afraid that if Jean and I came to the Queen's defense it might cause her more harm. Her accusers might say we had been bribed into lying for her.

If it had turned out that the Queen had been held at fault, I would have come to her defense no matter the cost to me. Or so I told myself.

Though the *Diamond Necklace Affair* was over, the strain of it had left the Queen badly saddened. Whenever I glimpsed her, she looked careworn.

The constant worry over Louis Joseph doubtless added to her depression. Everyone was aware that he was growing worse. He spent most of his time at Meudon, a rundown residence belonging to the Dauphin of France. The air was supposedly healthier there.

"How is the boy?" Pierre said to Henri. We would never have referred to him as *the boy* in the presence of any of the royals, but we thought him a sweet little lad. We all loved him. He was our boy, too.

"Not well," Henri said, taking off his chef's hat and running his hand through what little hair he had left. "The coughing sickness has gone to his bones, the doctor fears. His spine is twisting."

"Scrofula then. Even the name sounds sinister," Pierre said.

"At his coronation, the King's touch supposedly brings God's healing. It is said it cured many of scrofula."

"Doesn't seem to be working on his son. What good is the King's touch if it can't bring God's healing to the one he loves beyond all?" Pierre asked.

"Have you seen the King lately? He looks worse than the Queen."

"Sad days, these."

The months that followed were much the same. It was as if the strange dust that had hung over France had been replaced by a cloud of worry. We weren't even serving as many sweetmeats.

The birth of another child to the King and Queen did little to raise our spirits. Sophie, named after the aunt who'd died of dropsy, was not a healthy baby. Sadly, the Queen had put on weight and no longer moved as gracefully as a dancer.

One day blurred into another, my duties largely the same.

Apparently, Emilie did pay attention to the days as they passed. She woke me just before midnight, the kitchen deserted. The night quiet was eerie. Nevertheless, I preferred it to the roar of the fire in the foundry where I had considered bedding down.

"What is it? What's wrong?" I turned to her, raising myself on one elbow.

"Finance minister Calonne has told the King that the kingdom is so deeply in debt it will not recover."

"The King has known of the debt for many months now. Why are you so upset? Did Mr. Jefferson not bring any money to pay back France?"

"What would America pay it with? Mr. Jefferson even appealed to the King to let the new nation export tobacco to France. No way. That's the *King's* monopoly. Hear me, Jacques! The King was told the kingdom would *never* recover."

"Never?"

"Never. This is the beginning of the end. August 20, 1786."

She left me, coming and going like a wisp of dream.

The next morning, everyone was strangely quiet. Usually, there was so much gossip I felt I could carry a dipper around, collect it, and sell it to the highest bidder. That day, it was as though a wind had blown through the corridors and stolen the voices of all who worked there.

Emilie avoided my eyes as she removed some wilted greens from a basket.

Jean. Nothing would stop him from talking, I was sure of that.

I ran into him half way to the menagerie. He'd been looking for me, too.

"'ave ya 'eard?" Jean blurted.

"Yes," I answered. Neither of us needed to explain what the other meant.

"Pack your bags. We'll be leavin' 'ere soon."

"I refuse to believe the kingdom will not recover. Anyway, what would I pack? And I can't wear the King's livery in the streets. These fancy shoes? How far could I walk in them, even if they do fit?" I had grown into Lafayette's shoes, if ever they'd been his.

"There are some second 'and stores in Paris. Next time me uncle and me go I'll pick up some clothes for ya. Put your foot by mine, so I'll 'ave a measure." I did. They were much bigger than his feet. "Got any money?" Jean asked.

"Only the few coins handed me when we were in Annonay getting Singe to shake hands."

"Never mind. I'll get the clothes somehow."

I was afraid to ask how. "Hold on, Jean. What makes you think I want to leave here?"

"Maybe you don't now. But you will. Just you wait."

He turned heel and headed toward the menagerie. I had a lump in my throat as I headed back to see if they needed any help in the kitchen.

∽

Chapter 23

It didn't happen. Not then anyway. The kingdom was still intact. The King reigned. The Queen continued to be the subject of gossip.

Some said the King was just buying time with something called the Assembly of Notables. This body of men had not been called since the time of Henri the Fourth. I knew that if a king was named Henri it was a *long* time back. We were in the King Louis line now.

It may have been finance minister Calonne's idea, though with his hacking cough it seemed any opposition would blow him away. Whatever, reform was in the air. Reform? What kind?

Pierre and the exceedingly not royal Henri were carrying trays of apple tarts to the oven. "The King thinks he stands a better chance with the Notables than with Parlement," Henri said. I was glad to see they were helping each other. I followed behind them and listened. Pierre said, "He has to do *something*. The peasants are refusing to pay taxes. Not just new taxes. *Any* taxes. That's the only way they think the King will notice they are taxed beyond their ability to pay."

We had hope. Then.

Lafayette was invited to attend the Assembly of Notables. The King didn't want him. Lafayette was filled with the ideals of the American Revolution and spoke to the Notables of rights and equality. The King wanted to fix the tax system, not change the kingdom. He wanted the King's *word* to be law.

About all that happened was that the Notables agreed to disagree. The politics of France got even stranger. The Parlement of Paris decided it had the right to veto the King's decrees. That spelled *big* trouble. After much wrangling, the King told the Parlement, *It is legal because it is what I want.*

I heard Thomas Jefferson and John Adams were corresponding about their new nation's need for a Bill of Rights. If that happened, France would have something more to talk about.

A peg-legged man named Gouverneur Morris, who'd helped write the new nation's Constitution, was now stumping the streets of Paris. Morris had changed the wording of the preamble of the Constitution from, We the people of the States of New Hampshire,

Massachusetts, Rhode Island...to *We the people...* If France ever recognized that concept, even I could see that the King's days were numbered.

To add to the King and Queen's troubles, little Louis Joseph grew worse. The doctor prescribed an iron corset in hopes that it would straighten his back. The brave lad didn't cry, though he must have felt like a snail carrying its house on its back.

It made me so sad I decided to find Singe. I put a banana in my pocket and asked around for him.

He was huddled in a corner of his cage looking so un-Singe-like that I couldn't believe it was the same animal. He wasn't wearing his little red vest. Roused from his stupor, Singe jumped to my side of the cage.

"Hello, little fellow. How are you doing?"

He tilted his head from side to side, looking for all the world like he was considering how to answer. But he didn't chatter. Instead, Singe reached through the bars of the cage and took my fingers in his.

Chapter 24

Even the weather seemed to work against the King. A hailstorm in July shocked everyone. It even sent partridges to the great beyond. Bountiful countryside was reduced to desert.

Bread riots broke out, something that had happened a lot. Months and months of the dry fog that dimmed the sun so crops didn't grow well, years of drought—and now this. I pitied the bakers of Paris, who never knew if their day would be peaceful—or if the starving poor would attack them and steal what little bread there was.

Later in the year, an Assembly of Notables met again. Not much got done then, either.

America had still not paid the French soldiers who had fought in the American Revolution. America was short of funds, too.

The King grew more desperate. When I saw him walking the halls alone, I knew he was in trouble. He was no longer surrounded by people currying favor.

To discuss the future finances of France, the King agreed to call a meeting called the Estates General. The Estates General hadn't met since the early 1600's. The Notables would have it no other way. *Only the Estates General has the authority to change the tax system,* they insisted.

The only comfort I found was visiting Singe. The day I had located his cage, he'd taken the banana I'd brought him, peeled it, and ate it as if it weren't important, so I knew he was getting enough to eat. But was he getting enough love? Enough exercise?

I was glad to see that every time I went to see him, he chattered more. I tried to quiet him, so no one would come to investigate.

Once Singe plucked a button off my frockcoat and found the cord and the velvet pouch hanging beneath my undershirt. I grabbed the pouch, not wanting my father's ring to be picked out by his clever paws and thrown onto the bottom of his cage where my button now lay. No matter how much I tried, I couldn't recover my button. Singe refused to give it back. It was his plaything now.

I asked Emilie to find another button and sew it on my frockcoat. The button didn't match, but no one paid me much heed, so I pretended it did.

Though he was a rascal, I knew Singe's mischief was simply an expression of what he was—a monkey.

Chapter 25

In the year 1789, everything began to fall apart. Of course, we didn't know it at the beginning of the year. There were signs, of course.

The Clergy balked at any suggestion regarding their taxation. Since they represented the wealth of France, this was serious. Though some priests were as poor as peasants, the Church itself was quite well off.

Bread riots were worse than ever. *Winter* was worse than ever. Bent old ones muttered, "I've not seen it this bad since 1709 when the red wine froze in Louis the Fourteenth's goblet."

Jean came shivering to the kitchen door and snuck inside. By this time, he and Emilie were as close as he and I were. She waved him in the direction of the storeroom. I was huddled on a sack of rice with my blanket around my shoulders. I didn't have much to do. The King wasn't working in the foundry; the bakers were only making bread today; it wasn't time to collect the candle stubs.

Jean didn't have to open the storeroom door. I'd left it open to get whatever warmth I could from the kitchen. Emilie was making a salad of turnips. *Oh, no.* I didn't take any. I'd rather have chicken broth.

"Do you know what they're saying?" Jean asked.

"Probably not. I haven't moved from this place for an hour."

He plopped down on my bag of rice in hopes of absorbing any heat I generated. "They're saying people are boiling tree bark, even dry grass, for something to put in their bellies."

I remembered well the times I had to exist on chestnut gruel and shuddered.

"Rivers are frozen, and the mills can't grind. What little grain there is can't be ground into flour to make bread. Everywhere in the Provence region, men lie dead from cold and 'unger."

"That's just the misery you know of. Think of what we do not know. How are the animals doing?"

"We've stacked so much straw 'round them they can't possibly eat it all. They 'uddle in it for warmth." He leaned toward me, both trying to warm ourselves from the body heat of the other. His jacket was so cold I moved my arm away.

Jean sighed. "You know Necker is back as finance minister."

"He's from a *long* time back."

"And makin' things worse for the King. Necker 'as called for input on how the Estates General should be organized. When educated men are asked for their opinions, they give 'em. Loudly, grandly - or conspirator- conspiratorially," he managed to say.

"You seem to know everything."

"Me uncle has been keen on it all. Talkin' in the taverns till late at night. At least that keeps 'im away from me. I've no new bruises this week," Jean smiled.

The winter led to a tumultuous spring. Necker got his hands on the grain supply—supposedly to share it among all the people of France. The Third Estate, everyone of value who was not a nobleman or a Clergyman, didn't believe that. They thought it was a plot to starve them. Desperate people can be led to believe the worst. There are always those in a kingdom who will play on people's fears to gain power for themselves. I couldn't point my finger at any one person, but I knew they were out there. Jean suspected the King's cousin, the Duc d'Orléans, of plotting against the King. The kingdom seemed to be holding its breath.

By May, little Louis Joseph was rarely without fever. His spirit still glowed in his girdled body. When the Dauphin heard there was going to be a grand parade for the opening of the Estates General at Versailles, he wanted to watch. He was brought from Meudon for the show. For a good view, the servants moved his bed above the royal stables

I wished that I had known the Dauphin well enough that I could have watched with him, but Jean and I were on the cobbles like everyone else. Emilie joined us.

First came the guards, and then the grand robed bishops and abbots of the Clergy who were from the First Estate. The nobility, who were the representatives of the Second Estate, wore their ceremonial swords over their shining garments and pranced like peacocks. Even the representatives of the Third Estate were impressive in their plain black suits and tricorne hats.

"Blimy," Jean said. "I've never seen so many swells."

Emilie grabbed my hand. "This is a grand day for France."

I wasn't sure why she thought that, but I nodded.

When the Estates General finally got around to meeting, things didn't go well. Something about the way the King put on and took off his feathered hat. "Did the big diamond in the middle swing too much as he took his hat on and off? Were the people that jealous of the King?" I asked.

Jean explained, "There's protocol 'bout 'ow the King and the nobles put 'ats on and off that indicates when to stand, when to sit. That sort of thing. Of course, the Third Estate knows nothin' about that, so they sat and stood like crows flappin' over a cornfield. That Gouverneur Morris fella thought it as amusin' as a scene from a Paris opera."

"How do you know these things?"

"I don't just listen to me uncle. I turn me ear to any bloke doin' the talkin'. It's 'ow I get me facts. That Necker fella? Made a abys - abysmal speech. The Keeper of the Seals done the worst. 'e announced there were to be no dangerous reforms. The delegates thought, *Wat are we 'ere for if not to reform France?* That Keeper guy wanted to censor the press again. Ya know, the press just recently claimed the right to print anything they 'ad a mind to. They 'ave a mind to print a lot. I could paper me room with it."

"I've seen pamphlets. I'm surprised the incendiary words didn't burn the pages."

"And the King's speech? Forget it!" The only good moment for the King and Queen was as the royal couple was leavin' the delegates chanted, *Vive le Roi, Vive le Reine!*"

"Long live the King. Long live the Queen. At least something went well."

That was about all that went well.

In June, I found Pierre and Henri dabbing their eyes with the corner of their aprons. I approached quietly.

"That awful steel girdle didn't stop the spread of his disease," Pierre's voice cracked. "Probably made him more miserable."

"They took it off toward the end, you know. Some say he died of rickets instead. Who knows?"

The end! I rushed forward. "Is Louis Joseph dead?"

"Yes, boy, at last."

I rushed out of the kitchen. I had only seen Louis Joseph from afar, but I felt I had lost a member of my family. The Queen had already lost one child. Baby Sophie died before her first birthday. It seemed so unfair. I ran to Singe and hugged his cage. Singe came over and played with my hair, the touch of his small paws my only comfort.

༄

Chapter 26

I saw Madame Victoire approaching a narrow doorway in the hall ahead of me. She reached into her muff and pulled out a jar. I was sure it was the jar of butter. While she was fumbling to unscrew it, an idea occurred to me.

"Pardon me, Madame."

"Ah, it's you. Where have you been hiding all these months? I almost didn't recognize you. You've grown so tall and…uh…filled out. You are growing toward manhood, I see,"

"Yes, Madame. I have an idea, if you will permit me to say it."

She looked at me as if I were stepping beyond my bounds, but doubtlessly remembering my early rescues, gave permission.

"Perhaps if you would turn sideways, you might not have to use butter," I said.

"I've got most of the doorways buttered, so I slip through quite nicely, but I almost got stuck here yesterday. Apparently, I have rubbed the butter off this frame."

"If you should get stuck, I'm here to assist you."

"Still a clever one. Still a clever one," she repeated.

Madame Victoire put the jar back into her muff and approached the door.

I held my breath. She held hers. Madame Victoire had just about slipped through when she paused, looking bewildered.

Would I again have to get a running start to jam her through? I thought I was too grown up to do such a thing now, but I had gotten myself into this. I took a step back in preparation for a run when through she went!

"Jacques, you're a genius. I shall only have to carry butter to get through the narrowest of doors."

"Thank you, Madame," I bowed with genuine gratitude. No one had ever called me a genius before, and I doubted anyone would ever do so again. If all I had to do was use common sense, being a genius was easy enough.

I walked away, my steps light and my heart lighter.

The King and Queen did not have light hearts. They were terribly depressed by the death of their son. The grieving couple wanted to be left alone; the business of the kingdom could wait. They left Versailles and retreated to Marly-le-Roi. Politics came knocking. Instead of talking with some men from the Third Estate, the King turned them away. Woe unto him. Big mistake.

When the Estates General again convened, they declared they were now the National Assembly. The *National* Assembly. With America a new nation free of an English king, this implied that the wishes of a French King were no longer that important. Perhaps, not important at all.

This shook Versailles. Emilie threw down her towel and came to find me. Pierre, and Henri, and I were again baking cakes. In a château of over two thousand windows, even if the King and Queen were not in residence, that didn't mean the other royals wanted to do without. Now adept at putting on pink ribbons, I was frosting *petits four*.

"I warned you that August night," Emilie said. "The kingdom is slipping through the King's fingers. With the death of Louis Joseph, he has no will left to fight."

Emilie was only partly right. Urged by his brother, the Comte d'Artois, and the Queen, the King called a royal session.

The King did not come with hat in hand, so to speak, but he offered to consider changing things people didn't like about the ancient regime.

It was Jean who filled me in. He was more excited than I'd ever seen him. More than when the quagga broke free.

"The King, 'e offered to give up the royal pre-rog-a-tive to imprison someone indefinitely. He was even willing to stop the *corvée*."

Jean saw my blank look. "The *corvée* is forced labor on the roads. The bloomin' peasants 'ave to leave their lands, sometimes at 'arvest time, to work on the roads, poor sods."

So that's where the peasants had gone when I was still at home. Though forced to live as a peasant, my father had avoided the *corvée*. I sensed that my grandfather had been influential there. Perhaps he loved my father after all, and only pride had kept them apart.

"There's more," Jean went on. "'e might even change the 'ated tax on salt." The look on Jean's face made me wonder if his uncle slipped some of the animals' salt to peasants who found it cheaper to buy it from him than from the King.

Jean avoided the look in my eyes. "The King might be willin' to change the judicial system. And might not try to censor the tongue-waggin' press."

"Tongue-wagging? Newspapers and pamphlets don't speak."

"Don't be so pre-cise. Ya know what I mean. They'll say anythin' in those rags now."

"Sick stuff, if you ask me. Mostly lies, I bet. It's like striking a match to the kingdom's problems."

"Fannin' the flames, all right. Fannin' the flames." His double emphases made me wonder if he'd been hanging around Madame Victoire. I didn't think so. I'd never smelled any butter on him.

"'course the Clergy and the nobility will stay at the top of the social order like always."

I knew that even nobles could fall out of favor. My father had. My grandfather had seen to that.

I went to bed that night in a jumble of confusion.

॰

Chapter 27

More trouble. Once again back in Versailles, the King made the mistake of insulting the Third Estate. He ordered them to meet in a different place rather than meet in the same room with the nobility and the Clergy.

The Third Estate remained seated. They'd been kept waiting an hour before admission and didn't want to leave. They had been slighted over and over again in their lives, and they didn't want another day of it. A man named Mirabeau roared, *We will not leave unless forced at the point of bayonets.* Oh, no.

I found Jean and Emilie whispering outside the kitchen. When I approached, they stepped apart. What was going on? Jean was a year or so younger than Emilie, though older than I was, so I didn't suspect romance. What then?

This time it was I who asked, "You've heard?"

"There's more to come, I fear," Jean said.

"We were just speaking of it," Emilie agreed. "Making plans to..." Jean grabbed her hand, and she stopped talking.

In the awkward silence that followed, I decided that I should be the one to walk away. Perhaps there *was* a romance there.

"So it's to be a constitutional monarchy," Henri said to Pierre as he washed some blackberries. I edged closer, ignoring the apples I'd been slicing.

"A king who does not rule *can* be ruled," Henri said, wiping his hands on his apron. His fingertips left purple smudges.

"The King has alerted his troops here and in Paris. Some of them are refusing to serve under the King and are swearing allegiance to *the people*, whoever they are. Us, I suppose. I don't think my cousin in the guard has decided which side to take," Pierre said.

"We have it good here. Why should we want anything else if we're part of this *people*?" Henri questioned.

"Do you have any coins to rub together?"

"No, but the King doesn't have many either. He told the National Assembly that he may soon have to declare the kingdom bankrupt," Henri said. He popped a blackberry into his mouth as though it were his last.

Perhaps it was, for soon we heard that unruly mobs in Paris threatened to attack the Discount Bank and the King's treasury there (what little was left of it).

A few days later, when I was on my way to the bakery kitchen in the early dawn, Jean and Emilie ran after me. "The Bastille, the Bastille," they cried.

"Slow down. Catch your breath. What are you talking about?"

"A mob stormed the Bastille, stole one of Louis the Fourteenth's silver-inlaid cannons and let all the prisoners free," Jean managed to say.

"The last I heard, there were only seven prisoners."

"It's the symbol of the Bastille and the weapons that were stored there that they went after," Emilie said. "Since the fifteenth century, the Bastille has been the symbol of tyranny. The mob went mad. It was bloody awful."

When I got to the bakery, Pierre and Henri were talking about it, none too quietly.

Pierre said, "The King was awakened last night by his bodyguard. The King said, *What is it? Why are you waking me? Is it a revolt?"*

Henri piped in, "And the bodyguard said, *Sire, it is not a revolt, it is a revolution."*

I fell back against the wall as though I'd been shot. A revolution could last for years. Hadn't the one in America?

What to do? I was too young to fight, but who knew what age was too young? Which side would I take? The King's? The King who had been so good to me? Or the people's, of whom, I supposed, I was one? I walked out of the kitchen without asking what my duties might be that day.

I went to the menagerie. Jean was nowhere about, and the animals hadn't been brought new straw. I found a pitchfork and set to work. All the cages were unlocked, though the locks were still in place. It's a good thing none of the animals had bumped against them or they might have run all the way to Paris. Only the lion's cage was locked.

After hours of hauling straw and water to the animals, I was exhausted. I set myself one more chore. I oiled the rhino's hide as I held on to its strange hairy horn.

I went into the quagga's cage and patted his zebra-like neck. I imagined I heard a horse-like whinny, but I was never sure. I ran my hands over his brush-like mane. He let me, even though I had no apple to offer.

It was dark by the time I headed to the château. The kitchen was practically deserted. A few lone workers bent over their duties, but Emilie was nowhere in sight. I found some lukewarm broth, drank it, and headed to my storeroom bed.

Something was sticking out beneath my bags of rice. I lifted a corner of the nearest bag and saw a shirt, some trousers, a badly mended jacket, and the biggest shoes I'd ever seen. I slipped them on. They fit.

༄

Chapter 28

"The King 'ad to stand *below* the mayor of Paris and put the symbol of the revolution, that red and blue cockade, on 'is 'at," Jean said.

"No one is allowed to stand higher than the King."

"In the ancient regime, yes. But in modern day France? Better to go to a country that's through with its revolution than stay in one that's just beginnin'," Jean said as we walked near the Queen's little village. We wanted to be far from the château so that we wouldn't be overheard.

"I don't know. I just don't know." I was being repetitive. I must have worked in the château too long.

"We're too young to fight. And I...I don't want anything to 'appen to Emilie."

"Is it love?"

"'ow would I know? Me who's not 'ad much of it. But I fancy 'er."

I looked at him closely. His clothes were clean, his hair as neatly combed as his curls would allow.

My straight hair was longer than ever. With all the upheaval, Emilie hadn't gotten around to cutting it.

"I don't know. I just don't know," I repeated. "The King has been wonderful to me."

"By lettin' ya work in that 'ot foundry bangin' away?"

"I haven't done that for a long time. But don't you see? He took an interest in me. Taught me well. It's not his fault that he has lost heart. He seems beaten. The Queen is the one who has some fight left in her."

"Not so many people kissin' up to 'er as there was. People is tryin' to decide which side their bread's buttered on. If they 'ave any bread, that is. The nobles are runnin' scared. In the dark of night, I 'ear carriages rumblin' out of Versailles. To England? 'olland? Spain? Or trying to get on a ship to America like we should!"

"We don't have any money. Not enough to buy passage."

"So we'll sneak aboard ship. 'opefully, the captain won't throw us overboard. Maybe 'e'll let us work for our crossin'."

"But you get seasick. You told me that's why you never wanted to cross the English Channel again."

"Maybe the Atlantic will be smooth sailin'. What's the choice? Lose me 'ead or lose me lunch? If I 'appen to be in the way of an angry Frenchman wantin' to kill a noble, ya think 'e'll just wait for me to get out of 'is way? Me uncle says boats on the river Seine was swamped with people tryin' to flee. We need to go to Le Havre where the big ships are."

"How would we get there?"

"Me uncle said 'e'd take us in the wagon. 'e's joinin' *the people* and doesn't want to be bothered with the likes of me. The mobs is desperate.

Three years of drought, pitiful 'arvests.... They're like a wild beast ready to tear prey apart."

That scared me, but I said, "Let me think about it."

"Don't think too long. Emilie and I might take off without ya. France is a powder keg about to explode."

Chapter 29

The old rumor was circulating again. *The aristocrats will starve us.* The peasants stormed manor houses, frightened the nobility—and worse. It was called *The Great Fear.* I wondered if my grandparents survived, or whether they now lay dead.

One of the King's brothers, the Comte d'Artois, fled France—maybe in one of the many rumbling coaches that Jean heard in the night.

I was helping Pierre and Henri remove bread from the oven when we heard a great cacophony. Such noise! Prattling women. Screaming women. I put down my tray of bread and went outside in the rain. Jean and Emilie were already there, staring, huddled together. At least there was rain! But it didn't take me long to wish for a dry place to stand, though I savored raindrops on my tongue for a while.

"Five thousand women from Paris have marched to Versailles to tell the King of their plight—as their grandmothers did in the terrible winter of 1708-1709," Emilie said as I joined them.

"That was the winter when the wine froze in Louis the Fourteenth's goblet, wasn't it?" I said.

For once, Jean was speechless. I nudged him with my elbow and words spilled out of him. "Look at those Amazons. Some are so tall they must be men dressed as women. We should've gone to America when I wanted! This crowd 'as blood in its eye."

A group of women came forward. The guards stopped them, spoke to them, and let one woman inside.

"'er's goin' to tell 'is Majesty of their 'unger, I bet," Jean said, blotting the rain running down his nose with the back of his sleeve. The rain grew heavier, so we retreated inside. The farther we got from the eyes of the raucous women, the better.

I returned to the bakery and began to peel and slice apples for a tart. I was lifting the tart into the oven when some of the King's guards rushed in. "Give us all the bread. Gather all the grain and flour and bring it to the market women. Maybe we can save the Queen. They want to make cockades of her."

That was impossible, I thought, but I helped Pierre and Henri empty the kitchen of foodstuffs. We even threw in gooseberry tarts that Pierre had made the day before.

I went to my storeroom and removed the grain stored there. I wondered if the bags of rice should be included. Surely, those of us in Versailles must have something to eat. If we had to boil the contents of my bed, so be it. I kept one bag for a pillow and carried the rest to the mad women.

Shoulder muscles complaining, I lowered the last bag from the storeroom to the wet cobbles. The women were fighting over the bread like wild dogs. I saw Emilie watching. She was shivering. I hoped the rain and the weather weren't giving her a chill. Maybe it was just the shock of seeing the seething mass before her.

Demanding shelter before the intermittent rain turned the flour to paste, the women shouldered the sacks. One by one, the women retreated. How the women would get the heavy sacks back to Paris was beyond me. Doubtless, they would demand a wagon from the King. *Demand* it of the King? I couldn't believe what I had just thought. *No one* could demand *anything* of the King. Yet people were.

Around four in the morning, I heard the women shouting, "Kill her. Kill the Queen."

I ran outside. Why the Queen had become the object of their rage puzzled me. I never believed the gossip and lies about the Queen. She was certainly innocent of the *Diamond Necklace Affair*, but that was the least of what they were saying about her.

Emilie and Jean found me. "Set your eyes on Lafayette. He may save us all," Emilie said.

"Lafayette? Here? Which one is he?" I craned my neck.

"On the white horse there," Jean said. "Its name is Jean Leblanc. Lafayette's now commander of the National Guard of Paris. 'e's still loyal to the King. Filled with passion, 'e is. Wants France to be like America—with rights for the likes of us. I don't think the National Assembly expects such rights to apply to the poor peasants who live on *their* lands!"

The women surged forward in a wave of sour smelling flesh. Some of them smelled like fishmongers. I gagged.

Emilie learned toward me. "Don't show weakness. There is danger in a mob, even if it is a gaggle of women."

We watched the goings-on until we could stand up no more. Emilie and Jean went to their beds. I suspected Jean only made it as far as the menagerie before he found some straw and bedded down.

I sought the comfort of Singe. I'd not gone deep into the château when I heard cries within. The women had broken into the château!

Lafayette charged past me and into the King's apartment. A mob was running through the *Galerie de Glaces* upsetting statues, brandishing daggers and fish knives, ripping furniture and curtains. Was that the King's locksmith destroying that chair? The man turned my way as if he knew he'd been spotted. It *was* him! He looked at me as if I was about to become a *dead* rat.

I ran as far as I could and slipped behind a curtain. When I heard shouting in the King's chambers, I knew the Queen and her family had made it through the hidden stairway that led from the Queen's apartments to the King's heavily guarded one.

Gunshots! I shook so badly I thought my teeth-rattling would give me away. Something did. The curtain was yanked back in a flash. It wasn't the locksmith. It was an ugly woman, black hairs growing from a big mole on her chin, teeth the color of spoiled limes. She was on me in a heartbeat, her knife at my throat. I swallowed so hard the movement of my Adam's apple invited the thrust of her knife.

"What're ya doin', ya little fop? Why ain't ya joinin' us instead of toadyin' to the Austrian born Queen?"

"I don't work for the Queen, Madame." *Madame!* That was stupid. That title didn't apply to this smelly woman any more than it did to me. It shocked her, so maybe it wasn't stupid after all.

"Ya don't? Then what're ya doin' hidin' here?"

"I serve the King." The harridan lifted the knife from my throat. When she did, I bowed as deeply as I could. Startled, she dropped the foul-smelling knife. We fought over it, and she scratched me with her filthy nails. When I wrenched the knife from her, she thought I'd stab her! Instead, I handed the knife back to her and bowed. She was so stunned that she pocketed the knife and rushed to join the others. I collapsed on the floor. I was shaking so much I was sure the curtains would fall from their rods and the foundations of the château give way.

Lafayette ran past me, away from the King's chambers this time. Forgetting I wanted to see Singe, I followed Lafayette outside in the hope he could protect me. He directed the National Guard to various entrances of the château and restored some order. The women still milled around, shouting insults.

In full daylight, Lafayette staged a balcony scene. He kissed the King's hand as a symbol that the National Guard supported the King. Then he placed the revolutionary symbol on a bodyguard's hat to indicate the King's guard now belonged to France.

The crowd liked that, but they didn't stop their demands. They were determined that the King and Queen come with them to Paris

The King and Queen, their children and other royals, including the old aunts, were hastily bundled into carriages. I can't say they were escorted to Paris by the parade of women and National Guard. They were jostled and cat-called there as the rain continued to pour down.

The royals were forced to live in the Tuileries, a rundown palace not nearly as grand as Versailles. *As prisoners? So Paris could keep an eye on them?* No one seemed to know.

Those of us left in Versailles rattled around the empty halls looking shaken and pale. We had rice from my pillow for supper.

∽

Chapter 30

The days that followed were strange ones. No one knew what to do, where to go. Without the King's presence, we were lost.

The storeroom was practically empty. I no longer even had a rice bag pillow. Its contents had been eaten long ago. I lay my head on the clothes Jean had brought me when going to America seemed imminent. It was my fault we were still here. My waffling, *I don't know. I just don't know.*

Pierre and Henri left to seek jobs in Paris. With their skills, they could certainly learn to make brown bread.

Jean found me eying the empty sack that I'd once filled with candle stubs. Jean and Emilie and I took a walk just to have something to do. "A man from the National Assembly 'as been lookin' at the menagerie tryin' to decide what to do with the animals," Jean said. "I don't know wat's goin' to 'appen, but I know wat 'appened to the King. The poor bloke 'ad to come before the National Assembly in Paris dressed like a member of the *commons*. That's what the Third Estate likes to call itself now."

Emilie said sadly, "No more the hat with the glittering diamond. No more diamond buckles on his shoes. No more the kingdom at his feet." Tears glistened in her eyes.

The next day, Emilie and Jean were waiting for me as I left the storeroom. Two knapsacks lay at their feet.

Jean spoke first. "We're goin'. To America."

Emilie hugged me. "I don't want to leave you behind, Jacques. It won't be safe. I can feel it in my bones."

"Me uncle is waitin' with the wagon to take us to Le Havre. It's now or never, Boy-o."

"Give me a minute," I sighed. I walked into the storeroom, my shelter for so many nights. I took off the white stockings, the faded green livery, the big brocade shoes. I donned the clothes Jean had brought me. He'd chosen well. My wrists stuck out a bit too far beneath the sleeves of my jacket; otherwise, everything fit. I placed my neatly folded livery near where, so long ago, Emilie had rustled in the sack of old clothing to find something for me to wear. I took only the blanket Emilie had given me.

"I'm ready," I said when I came out.

Jean wasn't there. "What happened?"

"He'll meet us at the menagerie."

We walked slowly down the path I'd taken so many times before. The fountains were turned off. The statues seemed to shiver in the cold.

The paint of the menagerie was more faded than ever. It was never a show place in the time of King Louis the Sixteenth. I imagined it in the time of Louis the Fourteenth, paint newly shining, the glittering King walking past the lion's cage in his vest of diamonds....

When Jean joined us, my thoughts came back to this sad year. Jean's uncle Bertrand was waiting in the same wagon we had gone to Annonay in. Jean helped Emilie aboard, then hoisted the knapsacks.

We did not leave by the same gates I entered when I first came to Versailles. Those gates were held fast by an enormous lock. I hoped it was not a lock the King had made. How sad that would be.

I clutched the velvet bag beneath my shirt and watched Versailles fade from view. Had I dreamed my time there? No, Emilie and Jean were here, and there was...Singe! Jean was unbuttoning his shirt so the monkey could swing free. He clambered onto Jean's shoulders.

"Never knew who 'e belonged to. Don't know if they're still about. So I thought to meself, why not? Even if 'e belongs to the King, 'e's been left behind with no one to care for 'im."

I patted the top of Singe's head. He looked at my hand, expecting a hidden treat. "How did you get him out of his cage?"

"The lock was in place, but not locked. Did that once meself in the menagerie. Wondered if the animals would escape and run free, but they didn't. The menagerie is the only 'ome they know now." He scratched Singe's belly as the road stretched before us.

I smelled the sea before I saw it. It stretched to the curve of the earth. How unbelievable it looked to me. It was a vast blue that seemed to have no end. No wonder ancient maps warned of unknown waters, *Here be dragons...*

We thanked Jean's uncle for the ride and walked along the wharf, eying ships. There were so many it seemed impossible to choose which one would be on its way to America.

Some were brightly painted, others looked as if they'd never known a coat of paint. Some sails were battered, some masts were broken. How would we decide which one to risk our fate to?

Jean talked to some old sailors in a tavern. They gave us the name of a ship, the *Espoir*, that was bound for America. The name pleased me. It meant *hope.* And we might well need hope, for it was one of the ships that looked a bit bleak.

In the dark of night, when the sailor on watch had his back turned, we scampered aboard. There was no time to waste. No one wanted to make the long journey in the rough seas of winter. Especially Jean.

What lay ahead of us, I didn't know. I was as worried as I'd been on my journey to Versailles to find Emilie. But now I had companions to share my fate.

We'd not yet made our way far out to sea when Jean started retching over the ship's rail. One sailor asked another, *Who is that lad heaving his insides out?* That's how Jean was discovered; they found the rest of us hiding under a tarp.

The Captain put us to work. Emilie in the galley, Jean swabbing the decks, I in the Captain's quarters. Doing anything honorable anyone asked of me had served me well in Versailles. So I cleaned the Captain's looking glass, put the sextant in its case after he made navigational sightings, made his bed, shined his shoes, and brought him his food.

When Jean got used to the motion of the waves and our chores were done, the night was ours. We met to look across the starlit Atlantic. Singe walked beside us, trying out his sea legs. The rippling waves broke against the ship in primeval rhythm. We felt infinitesimally small in the vast space of sea and sky.

"What's that I smell?" Emilie asked.

Jean chuckled. "I swab the deck with vinegar water. Before I throw the water overboard, I give Singe a bath with it. Smells like a pickle, 'e does."

The three of us broke into gales of laughter. Singe looked up at us as if he thought he had strange traveling companions. Jean swept him onto his shoulders. Singe immediately started playing with Jean's curly hair and watched the waves with us.

Our hope lay in our friendship and the land far beyond the sea—America. Dr. Franklin had been right. I was young. No telling where I would go…No telling where *we* would go…

∽

Afterword

In this story, I tried to keep as close to the history of the time as I could. Jacques, Jean, and Emilie are fictitious, as are the pastry chefs. Some of the other characters are used fictitiously. I don't know if the "old" aunts were even fat! Poetic license is the terrain of the fiction writer, and I enjoyed being there. Some of my early readers thought that the quagga was a mythical animal. It is not. The last true quagga died in 1883. There is a project to bring the quagga back from extinction. See http://www.quaggaproject.org

About the Author

Jane Bradfield has written for newspapers and magazines, and is the author of two books. Her work has been published in several languages. Her first book, *Rx Take One Cannon,* is about the discovery of the small cannon a doctor thought the Texas Revolution was fought over. It's a funny detective story, covering two centuries, ending in the Smithsonian giving the cannon a nod.

All That Glitters is her first work of fiction. She is thinking of writing a sequel, *Beyond All That Glitters.* That book would continue the adventures of Jacques, Jean, and Emilie in Philadelphia, the temporary capital of the United States during George Washington's presidency. She lives in the heart of Texas with her family.

Made in the USA
Charleston, SC
27 January 2011